Terrence is being pulled into a war he wants nothing to do with. He has a choice to make — follow his alpha's orders and do the wrong thing or help the dragons and put himself and his family in danger.

Donahue doesn't know what to think when Terrence lands in front of the clan house and asks to talk to Elijah, but he protects him from the dragons who want to hurt him because of what he is. Luckily, Elijah is a good alpha, and in exchange for information, he agrees to take Terrence and his family in.

But Irwin leads the cockatrice clan with an iron fist, and he doesn't take nicely to four of his people running to the dragons. The dragons need to find allies, and fast. If they can't, Terrence and Donahue stand to lose their families.
And each other.

A Psychic is Worth a Thousand Words
Copyright © 2024 Catherine Lievens
ISBN: 978-1-4874-4114-2
Cover art by Angela Waters

Published by eXtasy Books Inc

Look for us online at:
www.eXtasybooks.com

A Psychic is Worth a Thousand Words
It's a Psychic World 6

By

Catherine Lievens

CHAPTER ONE

Irwin slammed his office door open and strode in. Terrence stayed as still as he could, afraid Irwin would notice him if he dared move. Everyone in the office was as tense as he was, hoping someone else would catch their alpha's attention.

It never ended well for those who did.

Irwin sat behind his desk.

Terrence wasn't sure why they were here, but he didn't think it mattered. Irwin was angry and wanted to take that anger out on someone. It easier to do so with the people Irwin felt belonged to him. He certainly wouldn't be able to take it out on the dragons, even though they were who he was angry with.

"We're attacking the dragons," Irwin declared.

Terrence sucked in a breath. He wasn't surprised, but he and his father had hoped Irwin would realize how foolish it was. Irwin had had to kill his own cousin because the man couldn't let go of the idea of making the dragons pay for whatever he felt they'd done to him. Irwin had to see how stupid this would be, right?

Evidently, he didn't. Otherwise, he wouldn't announce that the clan would be going after the dragons.

Terrence wasn't about to open his mouth and say anything about it, nor would his father. They weren't the top of the food chain here, and they couldn't afford for Irwin to be angry at them. The only reason they were at this meeting was Terrence's sister, and just thinking about her made Terrence want to strangle Irwin, which wouldn't be a good idea.

"Curt tried, and it didn't go well," one of Irwin's advisors said cautiously.

Irwin narrowed his eyes at him, but thankfully, it looked like he wasn't willing to shed blood today. "That's because he was stupid. There are ways to do these things, and he should have known better. He was obsessed with them and could only see revenge, but if we're going to get rid of the clan, we need to do so smartly. Going at it the same way Curt did will only create problems."

Curt had created problems for the clan, which was why he was dead. Irwin wouldn't have allowed him to put the clan in danger, and his obsession with the dragons had caused precisely that.

But he was gone now, and the clan was safe. Irwin had killed his cousin, and he didn't seem to care one bit about it. He hadn't shed a tear—not that Terrence had expected him to. Irwin was a cruel and hard man who thought emotions were for babies and women. He probably hadn't cried since he was a child, and he wasn't afraid of anything.

Or at least, that was how he behaved. Terrence was pretty sure Irwin was terrified of the dragons, but he would never admit it.

Terrence *could* admit he was terrified. He wasn't afraid of being afraid, especially when it came to Irwin. His alpha was a monster. Terrence and his family would already be far from here if things were different.

But they couldn't leave without his sister.

The door slammed open again. Terrence turned to it, ready to defend himself even though there wasn't supposed to be anything dangerous here. The clan was safe in their territory, or rather, they should be. The problem was when the danger came from inside the clan, especially from the alpha.

Irwin wasn't the danger today. On the other hand, Irwin's

aunt looked like she was ready to kill someone — specifically Irwin.

"What do you want?" Irwin snapped.

"What do I want? How can you ask me that after what you did?"

Irwin shrugged. "I did what was best for the clan."

"You killed my *son*." Elvira almost vibrated with anger.

Terrence wondered if this was it. Was she about to kill Irwin? He was the alpha, and he was strong, but she'd just lost her son, and her anger might give her enough strength to avenge him. What Curt had been doing had been stupid, and as far as Terrence was concerned, he'd deserved to die, but Irwin hadn't killed Curt because he thought it was the right thing to do and because it had saved people. He'd done it because Curt was annoying him and trying to take over his clan, which he couldn't accept.

Sometimes Terrence wished his clan would all kill each other and be done with it. Maybe if they did, it would be a safer place to live.

"I killed him because he was an idiot who thought he could take my clan from me." There was a threat in Irwin's voice. "If you're here to complain about that, you can leave. I did what I had to do, and I'd do it again if I had to." Irwin leaned forward. "In fact, I won't hesitate to do it again if anyone threatens me."

Irwin wasn't kidding. Everyone in the room knew it, including Curt's mother. It gave her pause, and Terrence expected her to apologize and leave. He was surprised when she didn't.

She straightened her back, and if looks could kill, Irwin would be deceased. Instead, he looked smug, but she didn't seem to care.

"I'm leaving," she said.

Irwin arched a brow. "Are you? It's about time. You

weren't welcome at this meeting."

"I'm leaving the clan."

Everyone in the room was silent. It was almost as if Irwin couldn't believe what his aunt was saying, which made sense. She'd always been a part of the clan, just like the rest of their family. No one left the clan. It just wasn't done. The only way to stop being a clan member was death.

"You know I didn't have a choice," Irwin said. He wasn't apologizing, but Terrence doubted Elvira would have stayed even if he had.

"I don't care what you believe. You killed my son, and you'll pay for that."

Curt's mother turned, not giving Irwin the time to argue. Terrence expected him to go after her or ask someone to grab her, but instead, he just sat there, and they all listened to the front door open and slam close.

Terrence exchanged a glance with his father. They'd talk about what had happened and how it might change their position in the clan later. It probably wouldn't change anything, but it would be good to discuss it anyway.

"Now that family drama is over, let's focus on how we'll take down the dragons," Irwin said.

He didn't expect Terrence and his father to participate, so they didn't. They stayed where they stood, hovering by the door, and let Irwin and his people start the conversation.

Terrence wished he could help the dragons. They were on the right side of the fight, and the thought of what might happen to them made Terrence feel sick. It wasn't right not to help, but what could he do?

He and his family were running out of time to save Natasha. They couldn't reach her, since she lived with Irwin and his family, and soon Irwin would force her to marry his son. She was still young, only sixteen, but Irwin wouldn't allow her to reach eighteen before she got married. His son had started making noises that she was going on seventeen and old enough to get married.

Terrence and his family couldn't allow Natasha to be forced to marry Eddie. The problem was that Terrence didn't know how to stop it from happening. Irwin was too strong, and Terrence didn't have allies.

Terrence frowned. Maybe he could have someone on his side. It was a crazy idea, but now that he thought about it, Terrence couldn't stop wondering if it could work.

He and his family needed someone who would help them get Natasha out and maybe hide them. They needed to hide long enough that Irwin would stop looking for them. It would take a while because the alpha was stubborn, especially when someone took something he considered his.

But Natasha wasn't Irwin's, and she certainly wasn't Eddie's. She was her own person, and Terrence had promised her he'd do everything he could to get her out of the situation she'd ended up in.

The problem was that he didn't know where to start. He only knew what would happen if he failed, and that wasn't something he wanted to think about.

But he might have to if he couldn't find a way out.

Donahue tried to focus on the movie, but it was impossible. The fact that he'd already seen it didn't help, but even more, his thoughts didn't allow him to do so.

They centered on the cockatrices and what they were up to. No one believed they'd take a step back and stop trying to attack the dragons. Curt might be dead, but it didn't mean the cockatrices had given up.

Donahue was curious to know what had happened to Curt. His body had been found, but how had he died? Donahue doubted it had been a natural death, which meant someone had killed him. It hadn't been the dragons, though. Elijah wouldn't have hesitated to admit if he'd been behind it.

But if not the dragons, who? Donahue wondered if his own people had killed him. What little he knew about Curt and the circumstances that had pushed him to fight the dragons told him that Curt wasn't someone most people liked. He'd been a monster and a user, and even though he'd been focused on the dragons, Donahue was ready to bet they weren't the only ones he'd hurt. He'd probably hurt his own people, too, which meant anyone could have killed him.

It wasn't his problem. As long as Curt was dead, he wouldn't create problems again. That didn't mean the dragons were safe, unfortunately. Even with Curt gone, Donahue was ready to bet they weren't out of the woods yet.

Something knocked against his shoulder. He looked sideways at his brother, who narrowed his eyes before returning his attention to the TV screen. Everyone else was staring at it, too. Donahue seemed to be the only one distracted, but he was sure that wasn't the case. The situation the clan was in was too dangerous and complicated. Everyone had to be worried.

But there was nothing any of them could do. Maybe worrying over it was the worst thing Donahue could do. There was nothing in his power to change the situation, and he wasn't the one in charge of the clan. That would be Elijah, and the dragon shifter knew what he was doing.

Donahue was glad he wasn't ın charge. He wouldn't have known what to do, and he'd have panicked. Most days, he didn't even feel in charge of his own life, even though he was thirty-seven. When he'd been a kid and a teenager, thirty-seven had felt like an eternity away and that by then he'd be an old man who would have his life in order.

He almost snorted out loud. If he could get his hands on his younger self, he'd give himself a good shake. Some days he might feel old, but he wasn't, and he definitely didn't know what he was doing with his life.

He didn't even have his own place anymore. After his brother Victor had been thrown into the mess between the cockatrices and dragons, it felt safer for everyone to move in with the dragons. Donahue had been on board because it had seemed exciting, and it was. Instead of a small apartment he hated, he now shared a massive home with a bunch of fascinating people. Having to live with his brothers wasn't a problem. There was more than enough space, and he'd always loved his family.

If only they weren't in danger. That was what worried him, and he couldn't help but wonder what would happen by the end of this. He needed his entire family to be alive and well when all of this was over, but would they be? Donahue had also made friends with a lot of the dragons and psychics who lived here, and he couldn't even think about losing one of them.

But a war was coming, and they'd have to deal with that.

"Stop wiggling," Olsen whispered between his teeth. "You're distracting me and everyone else."

"Sorry," Donahue said.

Maybe he wasn't in the right mood for movie night. He'd thought it would distract him, and he liked being in the middle of such a big group. He'd always loved his family, and he was delighted by the fact that it now included a clan of dragons. They weren't related by blood, but it didn't mean they weren't family. Donahue hoped that he'd be allowed to stay even after the mess with the cockatrices was over. He didn't want to have to find a new apartment. There was no going back to the old one, since he'd been renting, but even if he found the best apartment ever, it wouldn't be the same thing. He wouldn't be surrounded by so many people who made him feel like he belonged.

As far as he was concerned, having too much family wasn't

possible. He loved being surrounded by people who cared about him and who mattered to him, and he wanted it to continue.

But before considering the possibility of moving out, he needed to focus on the fight. The cockatrices wouldn't lay low for much longer, and when they struck, it would be war. It didn't matter that the dragons had done everything they could to stay out of it and that they wouldn't be the aggressors. They couldn't avoid it, and even if they won, they might still be in trouble.

Humans didn't look at groups of shifters fighting with a good eye. They wouldn't be happy about it. They already weren't, and they never hesitated to blame the dragons. Luckily, Elijah had a journalist friend who always wrote the truth, and he'd helped smooth things out recently.

But he might not be enough. Nothing might be. Even if the dragons won the fight with the cockatrices, they might have to fight humans, too, and that wouldn't be easy.

Nothing in the near future would be.

Terrence and his father stayed silent as they headed home. They were alone in the forest, but it would be too easy for someone to follow them and listen in to their conversation. It was much safer to stay quiet, so they did.

But Terrence could feel his father was tense. He understood why. They'd spent a few hours listening to Irwin and his advisors talking about the dragons and trying to come up with a plan to kill all of them, take their territory, and win the war Curt had started. Every option had been bloody.

Terrence shivered at the thought of what life would be if the cockatrices and Irwin won. Irwin had no respect for life and guided the cockatrices with an iron fist. If he took over the dragon clan, he'd do the same. Terrence thought it would be a miracle if Irwin allowed any dragon to live, but life wouldn't be good to them if he did, and they'd probably wish they were dead.

The thought of so many people dying, the dragon clan being destroyed, and what it would mean made Terrence want to throw up. He needed to do something, but what? His hands were tied, and nothing changed, no matter how many times he tried to find a way around it. Irwin was still in charge, and he still had Natasha.

They remained silent as they walked into the house. Terrence's father closed and locked the door, and they moved toward the kitchen. Terrence wasn't surprised to find his brother there. Joe had known Terrence and their father would be at the meeting, but thankfully, he hadn't been expected to participate. He was younger, and Irwin didn't think it was his place to be there. Terrence and his father wouldn't have been there, either, if Irwin hadn't been trying to keep an eye on them. He knew no one in their family was happy with what was happening with Natasha, so he was wary of them.

He was right to be.

"How did it go?" Joe asked as he opened the fridge.

He'd put dinner together since he'd been home for a while. It was nothing fancy, but then Terrence was the cook in their family. Joe and their father knew enough to cook meat and put together a salad, which was what Joe had done. Terrence's stomach growled, and he quickly washed his hands before sitting down. The food was already on the table, and when Joe grabbed a few beers and some water, they were ready to eat.

"He truly thinks he can win against the dragons," their father said.

He looked tired, like he had every day since Natasha had been taken from them. He'd done everything he could to convince Irwin to allow her to stay at home until she was ready to get married, but Irwin had seen right through him. He'd known that if they could, they'd take Natasha away, and if they did, his precious son and heir would lose his new toy.

Terrence gritted his teeth. He didn't want to think about how Natasha was being forced into this. Initially, he'd thought Irwin would oppose it, but he seemed eager to get his son married to Natasha, and Terrence eventually realized why. Eddie would be the alpha after his father, which meant he'd need a son to take his place after he was gone, too. Clearly, Irwin wanted that to happen as soon as possible, maybe because his son was an idiot. Eddie was as likely to get himself killed as he was to take his father's place, and if something happened to him, Irwin would need a new alpha heir. He'd never allow anyone who wasn't related to him to be in charge.

"Did they come up with a plan?" Joe asked.

"They bickered the entire time," Terrence told him as he cut a bit of sausage. "They don't have anything planned yet, but that won't last. They'll attack the dragons eventually."

The sound of Joe's fork hitting his plate was loud. "It's not fair. The dragons haven't done anything to us, and I don't understand why Irwin is going after them. They weren't even the ones who killed his cousin. *He* did that."

"He wants power," their father said in a tired tone. "If he takes out the dragons, our clan will be the strongest group of shifters in the area. That means we could take over the city, and even though there are many more humans than cockatrices, I don't think it would be an obstacle. Irwin knows what he's doing."

Terrence agreed, just like he agreed with his father that they needed to wait and see what happened. Joe was young, though, and it was too easy for him to allow his emotions to take over. Terrence was afraid he'd do something stupid, but he didn't know how to stop his brother. He was already trying to protect his sister while at the same time obeying Irwin's orders and doing his job patrolling their clan's territory. There was nothing more Terrence could give.

But he'd try anyway.

"I agree with you that it's not fair," he told Joe. "But we have to be careful."

"We've been careful this entire time, and it hasn't helped. Do you know how bad things will become if Irwin wins? If he takes over the entire city? Our life is already hell as it is, but it's going to be worse."

"We know that, but there's nothing we can do right now. There are only three of us, and Natasha is with Irwin and Eddie. I'm sure you can imagine what would happen to us and her if we stood up to Irwin."

Joe looked disgusted. "We still have to do something."

"We will. We just need more time. I promise I'll find a way out of this and do my best to save our family and the dragon clan."

But Terrence's best might not be enough. That didn't mean there wasn't something he could do, though. He didn't know the dragons, but he'd met some of them, and even more importantly, he knew Valerian. He'd done what he could to protect the psychic when he'd been here, and Valerian had managed to escape with the help of the dragons. Terrence had seen him recently, and he'd seemed healthy and happy. Terrence wasn't sure what Valerian thought of him, but he'd always tried to be nice, and maybe that would be enough for Valerian to ask the dragons to listen to him.

But what could he tell them? Could he really put his family in danger to save them? He didn't want to have to choose, but he might have to, and he didn't know which way things would go.

Terrence's first priority had always been his family, and that wouldn't change. He didn't want anything to happen to the dragons because it wouldn't be right and because things would become worse if Irwin was in charge of the entire area, but right now if he had to choose, he'd have to choose his family. Natasha needed him.

But without the dragons, Terrence might not be able to save her.

CHAPTER TWO

It was really fucking cold, and Terrence couldn't wait for his shift to be over. Today, Irwin had put him at the entrance to their territory, which meant he couldn't even shift and keep himself warm in his cockatrice form. Terrence was pretty sure Irwin had done that on purpose. He didn't like Terrence and his family, and Natasha was the only reason he tolerated them.

Terrence would never understand why Irwin's son had taken such a shine to her. There were many women in the clan, a lot of them age-appropriate for Eddie. Why had he noticed Terrence's teenage sister instead? Why was he so obsessed with her that he'd pushed his father into deciding they should get married? Or had that been all Irwin?

Terrence had never dared ask. When Irwin had asked him and his father to come to his office to tell them that Eddie was going to marry Natasha, they hadn't been allowed to say anything. Neither of them wanted it to happen, but Irwin was the alpha. He made the decisions, and it didn't matter whether his people liked it or not. They needed to follow orders, or things wouldn't end well for them.

Terrence and his father knew it would be too dangerous to oppose Irwin, so they'd found another way to keep Natasha safe. Initially, they'd convinced Irwin that Eddie and Natasha needed to start dating. They'd pointed out that Natasha was young and had never had a boyfriend. That had worked, maybe because she'd only been fifteen then.

But Eddie was getting impatient, and Terrence didn't have

to ask why. He knew what Eddie wanted from Natasha, and it took everything he had not to strangle the asshole every time he saw him. When Terrence and his father had pushed back, Eddie complained to his father, and Irwin decided that Natasha needed to move in with him and his family. He'd promised Eddie wouldn't do anything before they were married, but how was Terrence supposed to trust that?

He didn't. He'd been trying to keep an eye on Natasha, but now that she didn't live with him and their family anymore, it was almost impossible. He checked in on her as often as Irwin allowed, but eventually, they'd run out of time. They were getting closer to her seventeenth birthday, and Terrence suspected that Eddie had had enough of waiting. He wanted Natasha, and he'd already waited too long as far as he was concerned.

Terrence shivered at the thought of what would happen to his sister—and because he was cold. He had to find a solution, but no matter how much he thought about it, the dragons were the only thing he could think of. Maybe Terrence could convince them to help, but why would they? Terrence had been there the day Curt threatened them at their gate, so they knew who he was. Valerian might have put in a good word, but what if he hadn't?

Terrence had treated him as well as he could considering the circumstances, but he'd still kept him prisoner, and Valerian could be angry because of that. He hadn't seemed to be the few times they'd spoken, but his life had changed. He'd found a home with the dragons, and now that he was safe, it would be easier for him to realize that Terrence had been as much of an asshole as Irwin and Curt, with the only exception that he hadn't hurt Valerian physically.

The sound of a car approaching jerked Terrence out of his thoughts. He frowned as he watched it coming closer, wondering who it was. He didn't think Irwin was expecting anyone. Usually, when he was, the alpha alerted the people standing at the entrance. He could have forgotten, and Terrence was sure that if he had, it had been intentional.

The car stopped in front of Terrence, and he quickly moved toward the driver's window. It lowered, and he peered inside, trying to recognize the people in the car.

He'd never seen them before, but he recognized their scent. They weren't shifters like the people Irwin usually met with. Instead, they smelled of magic, making Terrence's stomach churn with unease.

"Yes?" he asked.

"We're here to see your alpha," the guy in the driver's seat said.

"Do you have an appointment?"

"No, but you can tell him the Guillory coven is here."

Terrence had heard of the name, so he knew they were one of the most destructive covens in the area. He'd never had to deal with them, but he could tell that trying to stop them wouldn't be a good idea. He wasn't planning to sacrifice himself for the clan, so he took out his phone.

No one had stood up to Irwin when he'd taken Natasha. No one had told him it was wrong. Terrence could understand. Everyone was protecting their life and their family, and they couldn't afford to worry about anyone else, but it still left him bitter.

He stepped away from the car. The mages were human, but he wouldn't put it past them to use a spell to listen in to the conversation. He tried to keep it as brief as possible.

"What?" Irwin barked when he answered.

"There's a car full of mages belonging to the Guillory coven at the entrance. They want to talk to you."

Terrence expected Irwin to tell them to fuck off. Irwin disliked magic users or anyone who wasn't a cockatrice shifter. He especially disliked humans, and Terrence hoped it meant he'd send the coven packing. As long as he didn't use Terrence to do it, Terrence would be fine with it.

But of course, he wouldn't be that lucky.

"Let them in," Irwin ordered.

"Are you sure?" Terrence asked, even though he knew he'd regret it. "They're sketchy."

"Do what you're ordered to do," Irwin snapped. "Guide them to my house. I want to see them as soon as possible."

"I'm the only one at the entrance today."

"I'll send someone else. Bring them here."

Terrence didn't have a choice. He'd known he wouldn't, but he still disliked this situation.

Why was the coven here? What were they going to offer Irwin? It couldn't be anything good if they'd decided to visit spontaneously, and Terrence was ready to bet it had something to do with the war between the cockatrices and dragons.

He'd been worried before, but now it was worse. If the coven stepped into the fight and supported the cockatrices, winning would be much harder for the dragons, and Terrence couldn't afford for them to lose.

He wasn't about to climb into the car, so he gestured at the driver to follow him and then started running. He wanted to shift, but there was no way he was putting himself in that vulnerable position next to the car full of mages.

Luckily, Irwin didn't expect him to stick around. His front door opened as soon as the car parked in front of his house, and Irwin stood there, staring at the mages. When he noticed Terrence, he waved at him to leave, so Terrence did.

But he didn't go far. He texted his father to tell him what was happening and what he was about to do, then he put his phone on silent and quietly crept along the side of the house until he was under Irwin's window. It was closed, but luckily, Terrence was a shifter. His sense of hearing was much stronger than a human's, and it would come in handy to spy on his alpha and the mages.

Terrence would probably pay with his life if anyone caught him, but he didn't see another way. He needed to know what was happening, and he could only do that by spying on Irwin and the mages.

Once he knew what they were planning, he would have to act. He couldn't afford to waste time anymore, and he might have to sacrifice something. He dreaded that choice, but he was pretty sure that if he didn't warn the dragons, they'd lose the war, and that wasn't something anyone should want.

Donahue wasn't a patient man. In fact, he hated waiting. There was nothing he disliked more than not being able to do anything and wondering what would happen next.

Saying he wasn't taking this situation well was an understatement. He felt like something was crawling under his skin, and even though he knew he was safe in the house, every little noise made him jump. He wasn't actually scared a cockatrice shifter could sneak in, but his nerves were shot. He was distressed and nervous and didn't know how to deal with it.

He wanted to do *something*, but instead he found himself pacing the length of the bedroom he'd been staying in since he'd arrived. He'd tried pacing in the living room but was kicked out because he was making everyone nervous.

That wasn't what he wanted. He didn't understand how everyone else could go on with their day without wondering what the cockatrices were doing, but that was his problem, not theirs. He needed to come up with something before the inaction drove him up the wall. It wouldn't take long at this rate—unless the cockatrices finally made a move.

But what could he do? He was just a psychic. He wished he could shift into something small and sneaky that could go into cockatrice territory and spy on them. Maybe if he could turn into a bird or an animal, he'd be more useful, but he was as human as they came. His only ability was that he could talk to ghosts.

He stopped. He could talk to ghosts. It wasn't a rare ability in his family, and they all lived here, so he wasn't the only one who could do so, but as far as he knew, no one was using their ability against the cockatrices. Elijah hadn't forbidden anyone to help. He probably didn't expect anyone to do something stupid like spying on the cockatrices, but Donahue wouldn't be the one doing that.

No, that would be a ghost.

He quickly left his bedroom in search of Kenneth, the ghost. If he knew Kenneth, he'd want to do something, too. His main goal was to protect his family, and as long as he was careful in case Curt's girlfriend was around, everything would be all right. Hell, even if someone saw Kenneth, what could they do to him? Apart from pushing him away, nothing, and even if they did push him away, he'd be fine. He'd just find himself far from cockatrice territory, but it wasn't like he needed to move there. He just needed to do a little spying.

Donahue was almost gleeful as he looked for him. Kenneth spent most of his time around his family, and since Donahue didn't want to bother Kenneth's wife, he went to look for Victor and Tim. Even though Kenneth looked as young as Tim was, Kenneth was Tim's grandfather. He'd died a while ago, and he'd been hanging around the house since then, with no one able to see him. That had changed after Tim met Victor, and he was part of the family again.

Donahue didn't know how that felt. He'd lost his grandparents on both sides, and none of them had stuck around and become ghosts. He didn't blame them. He had wonderful memories, and he cherished them. He missed his grandparents and wondered what happened after death, but it was too soon for him to find out. He had plans.

Plans that didn't include a war with a bunch of cockatrice shifters.

When he reached Victor's bedroom, he knocked and waited. He had no idea where his brother was, but usually he could be found training with other psychics. Valerian was still learning, especially when it came to his mage powers, but Victor insisted that all the psychics needed to know what they were doing, and he was right. Lindsey had never had any training, and Victor had taken him under his wing.

The door opened, and Tim peeked out. He smiled when he saw Donahue, and Donahue tried to look around him to see if Kenneth was there.

"If you're looking for your brother, he's in the library," Tim said.

"Actually, I'm looking for your grandfather."

"Oh. Well, I have no idea where he is."

That was the problem with ghosts. One couldn't call their cell phones and find out where they were. If Donahue wanted Kenneth, he had to look for him.

"What do you need from him?" Tim asked.

"I have a question."

Tim's eyebrows rose high, and since Donahue could see he had questions, he quickly waved at him and stepped away. "Anyway, thank you. Talk to you later."

He didn't want anyone else to be involved in case Elijah got pissed when he found out what Donahue was doing. Tim would probably be on board, but just in case, it was better if Donahue kept it to himself.

It took a bit of searching, but Donahue eventually found Kenneth in the garden. He was with his wife, who was bundled up in a heavy coat and sitting on a bench next to the house. Donahue didn't want to bother her, but thankfully, Kenneth noticed him and came closer.

"Isn't she cold?" Donahue asked in a whisper.

Kenneth smiled. "She's always loved the cold. She hasn't been here long, so you don't have to worry."

Tim's grandmother was old, and Donahue would never think of telling her what she could or couldn't do, but he decided he should keep an eye on her while he was talking to Kenneth. It couldn't be good for anyone to be outside in the cold, although since Donahue wasn't a dragon shifter, what did he know?

"I was looking for you," Donahue told Kenneth.

"Oh? What can I do for you?"

"I don't know about you, but I've had enough of waiting for the cockatrices to act. I can't spy on them and find out what they're planning because they'd notice me, but not you."

Kenneth slowly nodded. "Not unless Curt's girlfriend is still around."

"I don't know what happened to her after Curt died, so there's a chance she's still with the cockatrices, but even if she is, she might not see you. I doubt she's with the alpha, and that's who you need to spy on."

"He could have other psychics."

"Maybe, maybe not. There's only one way to find out."

Donahue wouldn't push if Kenneth thought this was a bad idea, but he seriously needed to do something. He wanted to protect the clan and his family and loathed feeling useless.

Kenneth grinned. "There is. I'll go to cockatrice territory as soon as I'm done here. I'll find the alpha easily, since I've already been there. Alphas always live in the biggest house."

"Elijah doesn't." As far as Donahue knew, he lived in a room that was the same as everyone else's.

"He's special. He never wanted to be alpha for power or prestige. He just wants to protect his people."

"And the best way to do that is to find out what the cockatrices are up to."

Kenneth nodded and went back to his wife. Donahue wasn't sure how long it would take him to find out what the cockatrices were up to, but at least now they were doing something.

"What was that about?" Olsen asked when Donahue stepped back into the kitchen.

Donahue jumped and pressed a hand to his chest. "You almost gave me a heart attack."

Olsen rolled his eyes. "But I wouldn't be able to annoy you if you died."

"Then you better make sure you don't scare me to death."

"Whatever. You're not going to die just because I surprised you, and you should stop being that dramatic. You should probably stop planning whatever you've been planning behind Elijah's back."

"I'm not planning anything." Donahue didn't think his brother would run to the alpha to tell him what was going on, but he didn't want to risk it.

"Sure you're not, and I'm the Pope."

Donahue grinned. "What should I call you? Your Majesty?"

"I said the Pope, not the king. You're ridiculous."

"And you shouldn't stick your nose into this."

"I might not be a psychic, but it doesn't mean the situation doesn't involve me. I live here with all of you, and you're my family."

The last thing Donahue wanted was to remind his brother that he wasn't a psychic. He knew that sometimes it bothered Olsen.

He wrapped an arm around his brother's shoulders and squeezed him close, laughing when Olsen grunted and pushed him away. "I promise I'm not planning anything. I just want this mess to be over as soon as possible."

"Pretty sure everyone wants that."

Hopefully, Kenneth would find something that would help them win this fight. Otherwise, Donahue would be back to square one, and he'd have to come up with another plan.

Terrence's heart raced as he crouched outside his alpha's window. He heard Irwin walk into his office, and he wasn't surprised when he didn't tell the mages to sit down. Terrence could imagine the scene in the office. Irwin was no doubt staring at the mages, trying to make sense of their presence and to read their body language.

"What do you want?" Irwin eventually asked.

"You're not even offering us a seat?" a woman asked.

"I don't care if you sit down or not. I want to know why you're here."

There was the sound of someone walking, then the chair in front of Irwin's desk creaked. It always did when someone sat in it.

"My name is Natalina. I'm sure your man told you we're here on behalf of our coven."

"He did, so now tell me what you want."

"So impatient. We're here because Curt contacted us. Since you're the alpha, he has to be your cousin. He mentioned you."

"He's not here anymore."

"We saw the news," a man said.

"Then what are you doing here?"

"Your cousin offered us something," Natalina said. "We've been looking for this person for a long time, and Curt would have handed him to us in exchange for help getting rid of the local dragon clan. We still want this person, so if you can give him to us, we'll help you instead of Curt."

"Why would you do that?" Irwin sounded wary.

Terrence wanted to scream at him to say no, but not only

would Irwin kick his ass if he found out he was spying on him, he'd probably say yes to what the mages had offered just because Terrence didn't want him to. He could be incredibly petty when he disliked someone.

"I told you. We've been looking for a man called Valerian. Your cousin said he had him."

"He was taken away. Curt didn't know what he was doing, and he was unable to keep him here."

"That's a pity. Do you think you could get him back? Do you know where he is?"

"With the dragons. If you want that guy, you're going to have to get him from them."

"Then it looks like we have the same enemy. Working together will probably make things easier for both of us."

"And you just want him?"

"Yes."

"No payment of any kind from me or my clan?"

"No payment, and we don't want anything you might recover when the dragons are defeated. You can have their home and their territory. We just want Valerian."

Terrence felt like he was about to throw up. He didn't know why these people were here and why they wanted Valerian so badly, but Valerian was special. The fact that this coven was here for him meant that he and the dragons were in danger.

Irwin had been dangerous to the dragons before. Now, he might just be invincible. Terrence had never dealt with a coven, and he didn't know what they could do, but he'd heard of these people. They were the most powerful coven in the area, and they were ruthless and never hesitated to burn their enemies to the ground.

He needed to do something. He had to warn the dragons that the coven was here and ready to help Irwin and that the dragons needed to be careful and come up with a plan to fight both the cockatrices and these new mages.

There was nothing Terrence could do to prevent them from attacking the dragons. He was only one man, and he wasn't powerful enough. He couldn't even protect his own sister.

The only thing he could do was let the dragons know what was going on. He'd been afraid to do so until now, but he no longer had a choice.

None of them did. Curt had started a war, and Irwin was bent on finishing it. No matter what happened, people would be hurt and die. If Irwin won this war, life would be worse for everyone in the area. The dragons needed to win, and Terrence might be their only way to do so.

CHAPTER THREE

Terrence had been thinking about what he'd heard yesterday the entire morning. He couldn't afford to waste time if he wanted the dragons to be prepared when the coven attacked them, which meant he needed to do something now.

He couldn't without talking to his family. Natasha wasn't here since she was stuck living with Irwin, so the only people Terrence had to talk to were his father and his brother. He suspected they'd try to stop him, but he didn't feel he had a choice. The dragons needed to know that the coven was working against them and that they would face both mages and cockatrice shifters. Otherwise, they were doomed to fail.

Terrence waited until the three of them sat around the lunch table. He was so nervous he could barely eat, so he didn't even try. As soon as they were all there, he started talking.

"A bunch of mages visited Irwin yesterday," he declared.

His father nodded. "I heard about that. Do you know what they wanted?"

"I do. I spied on them and Irwin in Irwin's office. They don't know I was there," he quickly reassured his father and Joe. "They didn't hear or see me, and I left without anything happening. Irwin was normal with me today, so please don't worry."

Joe snorted. "Don't worry? You spied on Irwin. You know what happened to the last person who did."

Terrence remembered all too well and wished he didn't. "I didn't have a choice. I needed to know what was happening, and I was right to be worried. These people were here for Valerian."

"That weird guy Curt kidnapped?"

"He's not weird. He's a psychic and a mage."

"Whatever. Why did they want him?"

"I don't know." And Terrence didn't think it mattered. The only thing that did was that the coven wanted Valerian enough that they were ready to ally themselves with the cockatrices and attack the dragons. "But they told Irwin they want to work with him. They'll support him when he attacks the clan, and they'll take Valerian. It's the only thing they want, so you can imagine how gleeful Irwin was."

"This is going to be a problem," Terrence's father said.

"It is. Irwin was careful before because he knows how powerful the dragons are, but with the mages backing him, he's going to want to attack soon. The dragons won't know what hit them." Terrence sucked in a breath. "Unless someone tells them."

"You can't," Joe interjected. "It's too dangerous. Irwin will kill you if he finds out about this, and now that he has a coven working with him, who knows what they can do to you."

"I'll be careful. It's not like I'm forbidden to leave cockatrice territory. Irwin doesn't have to know I went to the dragons."

"What if he finds out? We already lost Natasha. I can't lose you, too."

The last thing Terrence wanted was to hurt his family, but he was trying to save all of them. This was the only way he could think of to do so. "We haven't lost Natasha. I was thinking of asking the dragons to take us in and help us rescue her. Maybe if I give them the new information about the coven, they'll be willing to help us with Natasha."

"What if they kill you? You're a cockatrice shifter. You're their enemy."

"I haven't done anything to them personally, and I'm sure that if I talk to Valerian, he'll convince them to listen to me."

Joe narrowed his eyes. "Nothing you can say will change their mind."

Terrence shook his head. "I need to do this. It might be our only chance to win this war and get Natasha back."

"You're not going to say anything?" Joe asked their father.

He hadn't been eating, either. He'd been listening, and while he looked worried, he shook his head. "Terrence is right. We need to warn the dragons if we want them to have a chance to win this war. If they lose, everyone's life will be hell, including ours. Natasha will have to marry Eddie, and no one wants that to happen. We can't help her on our own, but with the dragons' help, we'll be able to get out of here. Even if they don't want to help when it comes to her, we can't afford for them to lose the war."

Terrence got to his feet. "I'll go now. I'm off shift today, and Irwin won't expect to see me until I visit Natasha tomorrow."

It was Terrence's turn. Irwin was being stingy while allowing them to see her, but they'd all insisted. She wasn't a prisoner in Irwin's house, or at least, she wasn't supposed to be. If Irwin didn't want the situation to look like he was forcing her to marry his son—and he was—he needed to allow her family to see her. That was the only reason they could check in on her, and Terrence hoped he'd have good news after talking to the dragons. Even if he didn't, he wanted Natasha to know what was happening. She wouldn't be part of the war but was still involved.

Joe looked like he might stop Terrence, but instead, he pushed away from the table and stormed out of the kitchen. Terrence's father sighed and got to his feet to clean the table. When Terrence started to help him, he shook his head.

"You need to go. I'll deal with Joe and make him see this is the only thing we can do."

"He's worried."

"We all are. We might not have lost Natasha, but she's not with us right now, and I couldn't stand it if something happened to you or Joe. Please, be careful."

"I promise I will be." Terrence's goal was to save his family and reunite them. He would be of no use if Irwin killed him.

But even if he was, he needed to do this. It was the only way to keep everyone safe, and if something happened to him and he was killed, it would have been worth it to know his family was safe.

He just hoped the dragons didn't kill him on sight.

He left the house, eager to get started. He'd get there quicker if he shifted, but he needed to be careful. If someone saw him fly away, they might be curious and tell Irwin about it. Terrence knew the perfect spot from which to fly away, but he needed to be careful.

He walked deeper into the forest, keeping an eye and an ear open to ensure no one was following him. Once he was sure he was alone, he quickly stripped, loaded his clothes into the cotton bag he'd brought along, and looped it around his neck. He shifted and stretched his wings, wishing he were doing so for another reason. It had been a long time since he'd flown because he wanted to. There was no pleasure in doing so now. Instead, he could only feel fear and urgency.

He prayed the dragons would help. He didn't know what he'd do if they refused. They might even take him prisoner, but that wasn't something he could consider because if he did, he'd be too afraid to go to them, and he couldn't avoid it.

He realized he should have planned better when he landed not far away from the gate of the mansion the dragons lived in. He hid behind a tree as he quickly dressed, but as soon as he stepped closer, two guards appeared on the other side of the gate.

Maybe Terrence should have tried to find a way to contact them before showing up in their territory. The guards looked like they were about to eat him without giving him a chance to explain what he was doing there.

He cleared his throat. "I have information on what the cockatrices are planning."

"*You're* a cockatrice," one of the guards said. Her tone dripped with scorn.

"I am, but I'm not on their side. I need to talk to Valerian, please."

Terrence had little hope that these two would listen, but he was here now, and there was no going back. He didn't know what would happen next but prayed the dragons would listen to him.

If they didn't, they would all die.

Donahue wished he could do more to help Kenneth, but he wasn't a ghost, which meant he was stuck at the house. He tried to relax and act like nothing was wrong, but it wasn't easy. Once again, he couldn't focus on whatever his brother had put on the TV. His attention kept returning to the window as if he might see Kenneth through it.

The sound of someone running at the entrance made Donahue perk up. He didn't expect Kenneth to run into the house, and he knew it couldn't be a ghost when Olsen looked up, too. If Olsen could hear it, it had to be a human being.

Donahue got off the couch and went to see what was happening. Everyone was on edge, so he wasn't surprised when half of his family followed him. Valerian and his boyfriend, Cooper, were there, too, and Cooper looked ready to take on whoever was attacking.

It was kind of sad that they all believed someone was attacking, but that was how their life was at the moment.

"What's going on?" Cooper asked.

The two guards who appeared from deeper inside the house ignored him and rushed out the door. More arrived, and Donahue had to resist the urge to follow them. He wanted to go out there and see what was going on, but he knew better. Instead, he waited with everyone else.

When more guards came, Donahue decided he had enough. He followed them, ignoring his brothers calling for him to come back.

"I want to see what's happening," he told them over his shoulder.

He wasn't surprised to see Olsen, Roslin, Cooper, and Valerian following him. They wanted to know, too. Donahue would be shit out of luck if the house was under attack since he couldn't shift into a massive dragon, but he could still help warn everyone else inside the house.

There was a commotion at the front gate, which was pretty much what Donahue had expected. He didn't know what else to expect, but he was relieved to see that the gate was still standing. As he walked closer, it opened, and several guards rushed out. Whoever was on the other side tried to make a run for it, but they grabbed them and dragged them inside.

That was when Donahue realized he knew who was at the gate. He recognized the guy because he'd been here that time the cockatrices had confronted the dragons.

It wasn't smart for him to be back, especially alone.

Valerian cried out and rushed forward. Cooper was right behind him, swearing up a storm, and since they were running, Donahue decided he was going with them. He followed as the man was pushed to the ground. He tried to get up, but one of the dragon guards grabbed his shoulder and forced him to stay on his knees.

"Let him go," Valerian yelled before reaching them.

The dragons looked at him like he was nuts. "He's a

cockatrice shifter," the dragon holding the man on the ground said.

Now that he was closer, Donahue recognized the guard, too. He didn't like Jamison much, but they weren't close and barely knew each other. What he was seeing right now didn't endear the dragon shifter to him, though.

"He's a friend," Valerian argued.

"He's a cockatrice shifter," Jamison repeated as if he thought Valerian hadn't heard him the first time.

Valerian shook his head and moved closer to the cockatrice shifter. Jamison growled, which caused Cooper to step in front of Valerian. Donahue did the same, even though Cooper had the advantage. He was human, but he was also dead. Donahue didn't fully understand how Valerian had managed it, but he'd given Cooper his body back, or at least, *a* body. Cooper couldn't die, even when he was wounded. A dragon shifter could probably hurt him badly, but he'd heal from it.

Valerian wouldn't, and neither would Donahue, which was why it had been stupid to follow Cooper's move. They moved forward, pushing Jamison away from the man while at the same time making sure to stay in front of Valerian.

"Get away from him," Jamison snapped.

Valerian ignored him. He crouched next to the cockatrice shifter, gently touching the man's chin. He tilted it up so everyone could see the blood trickling from the cockatrice shifter's mouth.

"I'm sorry," Valerian murmured.

The cockatrice shook his head. "I should have known better than to come here unannounced."

"Why did you?" Donahue asked.

"Terrence is a friend," Valerian said, glaring around. "If any of you hurt him again, I'll make sure Elijah knows and makes you pay."

Jamison's growl was deeper and louder this time. "How

dare you threaten me in my own home?" he asked, stepping back toward Valerian.

Donahue knew it was stupid, but he still stood shoulder to shoulder with Cooper, shielding Valerian and the cockatrice shifter from Jamison. Everyone else was staring at them as if waiting to see what would happen and who would win.

Donahue had no doubt that Jamison would if there was a fight. He only needed to shift, and he could flatten both Cooper and Donahue like pancakes. Cooper would survive, although Donahue wondered how much damage his body could take before it fully broke down. He was more worried about what would happen to his fragile human body, though.

Unfortunately, Valerian didn't seem to have gotten the message that he needed to keep his mouth shut.

"Elijah knows who Terrence is," he said from behind Donahue and Cooper. "He'll be pissed if you hurt him."

"He's a cockatrice shifter," Jamison roared.

Everyone else took a step back as if they expected him to shift and start stomping around. Donahue kind of did, so he carefully retreated closer to Valerian. He didn't want anything to happen to Valerian, who was a friend, so maybe if Jamison shifted, Donahue could distract him while Valerian ran.

One look was enough to tell him that Valerian wouldn't be going anywhere without his friend. Donahue had no idea who Terrence was, but now that Valerian had mentioned his name, he remembered that Valerian had said that Terrence was the only cockatrice shifter who hadn't been cruel to him while he'd been there. He hadn't exactly helped him, either, but after Valerian had spoken a bit about his experience with Curt and the cockatrices, Donahue thought he understood. If Terrence had any family, he had to be terrified for them. It made the fact that he was here on his own especially puzzling.

He wouldn't be able to tell anyone anything if Jamison

tried to kill him, which would be a pity. Terrence might be on his knees and bleeding right now, but Donahue couldn't deny how handsome he was. He looked tired, but his shoulders were broad, and his body was well-built. He didn't wear a jacket, which was the only reason Donahue could see it. His sweater was thick enough that Donahue had to use his imagination for a few spots, but he didn't mind.

Terrence had brown hair cut short and brown eyes that were wide with fear. Donahue wanted to reassure him, but he wasn't sure he trusted this guy the way Valerian did. Valerian was the one who knew Terrence best, though, so Donahue decided to trust him. If Valerian said Terrence was here for a good reason, he was probably right.

"Get away from him," Jamison said.

"You're going to have to hurt me if you want to hurt him," Valerian snapped back.

Donahue groaned. "Please don't give him ideas."

Valerian was already shaking his head. "I won't let him or anyone else hurt Terrence. Did someone advise Elijah of what was happening? Because he'll want to know what Terrence has to say."

"That cockatrice has nothing to say," Jamison spat out. "My brother died because of him."

Donahue was pretty sure he meant that his brother had died because of *a* cockatrice shifter. Donahue hadn't seen Terrence anywhere when they'd attacked, although he could be wrong. He was only human, so he'd been locked up with the others.

But he doubted Terrence would be here if he'd been part of the attack. Whatever the reason for his presence, it had to be important and dangerous. Why would Terrence put himself in this situation otherwise?

Clearly, coming here had been a bad idea. Terrence should have found another way to contact the dragons. He hadn't, and now, he risked getting killed. At the very least, it seemed he was about to end up in the middle of a fight, and he didn't know what to do.

He was relieved that Valerian seemed to be on his side. The psychic was yelling at the dragon who'd thrown Terrence to the ground, and while Terrence was grateful for the support, he also wanted to tell Valerian to be careful. Valerian lived with the dragons, but it didn't look like the one he was yelling at liked him much.

Terrence wouldn't be surprised if the guy shifted, but he hoped that wouldn't happen. He had to talk to the alpha, and being in a fight would make everything more complicated. The problem was that he'd already asked to talk to the alpha, but he was nowhere to be seen. These people didn't understand the urgency, and they wouldn't unless Terrence blurted out what he'd heard yesterday.

He knew better than to do that. He had no idea who he could trust. Hell, he wasn't even sure he could trust the alpha. He didn't feel he had a choice, which was why he was here. His presence might not be enough, but he would do everything he could to at least pass on a message. Valerian needed to know that the coven was hunting him. Even if this ended in a war, Terrence wanted to help Valerian. It was the least he owed him after everything that had happened.

He didn't want anything else to happen to Valerian, so he stayed where he was on the ground and tried to make himself look as harmless as he could. "I'm not here to fight, and I wasn't here when your clan was attacked. I wasn't on Curt's side," he explained.

The asshole dragon growled and tried to get closer, but Valerian wasn't the only person helping Terrence. Two other men stood in front of him and Valerian, and while Terrence didn't understand why they were, he was grateful. They were keeping Valerian safe, and by doing so, Terrence. They probably didn't care about him, but Valerian seemed to, even though it didn't make sense.

"Enough," someone snapped, causing everyone to stop talking.

Terrence didn't understand what was happening right away, but when he glanced up, he saw that the people who had crowded around him, possibly to watch him die, were stepping aside.

It didn't take long before the alpha appeared. Terrence recognized him from when he'd been forced to follow Irwin here to demand Valerian be returned to him.

The alpha was on his own, and he looked almost regal. He definitely looked like the alpha he was, with broad shoulders, a straight back, and a square jaw. The way people looked at him told Terrence that he didn't rule with fear and cruelty like Irwin. Everyone was respectful and deferential but didn't cringe or try to hide. They obviously knew that whatever was happening, their alpha would be fair.

Terrence hoped it would extend to him, even though he wasn't a member of the dragon clan.

Now that the asshole dragon was distracted, Terrence got to his feet. Terrence nodded at Valerian, and Valerian gave him a tight smile. Terrence expected him to step away now that he was safer, but Valerian stuck to his side, raising his chin as if ready to challenge his alpha.

Terrence hoped he wouldn't do something that stupid. Valerian was human, and it would be too easy for the dragon alpha to hurt him. From everything Terrence had heard, he doubted that would happen, but still.

He moved and placed himself slightly in front of Valerian. He heard him huff, but he ignored him and focused on the man who came to a stop in front of him. The two guys who'd come with Valerian scrambled to step aside, and Terrence found himself face to face with a man he'd been told to avoid at all costs.

"What's going on here?" the alpha asked.

"Elijah, you have to listen to him," Valerian said as he tried pushing Terrence to the side.

Terrence didn't move. If anything bad was going to happen, he wanted to be sure Valerian wouldn't be hurt. He didn't care how huffy Valerian was.

"Listen to him?" Elijah asked.

It was time for Terrence to do what he'd come here to do. "My name is Terrence, and I'm a cockatrice shifter. My alpha is Irwin, and while I understand he's your enemy, I need you to listen to me. Irwin isn't a good alpha, and many of us don't want to follow him. We don't have a choice because he threatens our families."

Terrence's thoughts went to Natasha. He needed to find a way to get her away from Irwin and Eddie, and he would. He just wasn't sure if he'd have the support of the dragons yet.

But before he could think of her, he had to convince Elijah to give him a chance. He just needed to explain what was happening. Surely, Elijah would realize that Terrence was on his side.

"He wants to get rid of you and the clan, but he's been wary because he knows how powerful and strong you are," Terrence continued. "That's why he's been waiting, but yesterday, he had a visit from a bunch of mages. They belong to the Guillory coven, and since I spied on them, I know they're looking for Valerian. They told Irwin that as long as they could have him, he could have everything else after the fight against you. They offered their support, and he agreed. You have an entire coven of mages coming for you."

Terrence felt slightly out of breath, but he was done. There were details he needed to tell Elijah, but now the alpha knew why Terrence was here. He was aware of the danger coming for him and his people, and he'd be able to keep them safe.

Terrence just hoped he'd keep him and his family safe, too.

Elijah was silent for a long moment. Terrence was afraid to ask what he was thinking. He was pretty sure he didn't want to find out. He just needed his family to be safe.

"Take him inside," Elijah ordered.

Terrence panicked. He couldn't afford to be taken prisoner. He needed to go back as soon as possible.

"Please," he begged because he was ready to do pretty much anything right now. "I have to go back before Irwin realizes I'm gone. He'll hurt my family."

Elijah didn't even look at Terrence. He didn't say anything as the asshole dragon from before stepped forward to grab Terrence. Thankfully, Valerian wasn't the only one who seemed to think he was out of bounds. One of the guys from earlier placed himself between the asshole and Terrence, and by the time the asshole pushed him aside, two dragons had already grabbed Terrence.

It wasn't looking good for him, but at least he wouldn't risk getting killed on his way to whatever cell they were going to lock him in.

"Don't let him hurt my family," Terrence said.

He wasn't surprised when Elijah didn't answer. He might not be as cruel as Irwin, but he was still an alpha. His job was to protect his people, and Terrence understood that since he was a cockatrice shifter, he was a danger to the dragon clan. They had no way of knowing if he was telling the truth or if he was trying to play them. They had no way to know that Irwin truly would hurt his family if he found out about this.

There was nothing Terrence could do as the two dragons pulled him away. He looked back, watching the gates and his freedom disappear as he stumbled.

What had he done? He couldn't allow this to happen. He'd

told Elijah what he'd come to say, and he needed to go home. There was only one way he could think of to do so.

He pushed the two dragons away and shifted.

Donahue wasn't surprised when the cockatrice shifter started shifting. He would have done the same if he'd been in the man's shoes. From everything Donahue had heard, it looked like Terrence had come here to warn Elijah and Valerian about what was happening between the cockatrices and this coven. Donahue didn't fully understand why Terrence would do that, but he had, and Donahue didn't think he was lying.

Terrence had only come to warn the dragons, and now that he had, he wanted to go home to protect his family. Donahue had a hard time imagining an alpha hurting his people, but at the same time, when he thought of Irwin, he could see it. The man had killed his own cousin. What would he do to the family of a man who'd betrayed him?

"Are you sure about this?" Donahue asked as he shuffled his feet until he was closer to Elijah.

One of the dragons who'd been escorting Terrence inside had jumped onto his back, wrapping his arms around Terrence's neck. The other one shifted, and even though Terrence was impressive in his cockatrice form, there was no doubt the two dragons would win if he continued fighting.

Donahue had seen his fair share of cockatrice shifters when they'd attacked the house, and Terrence looked like them. He supposed that the dragons also looked very much like each other, although their colors were different. The same seemed to go for the cockatrices.

Donahue remembered the wings, the tail, and the giant beak. He'd expected cockatrices to look like giant chickens, but they were more similar to a dragon, even though they did have feathers. Terrence's body belonged to a bird, but his wings were leathery, like a dragon's. Maybe cockatrices were born from dragons and chickens.

Donahue almost laughed at the thought, but he knew better than to get anyone's attention, especially for something so stupid. Besides, what was happening in front of him wasn't funny. When Terrence tried to fly, the dragon who had shifted closed her jaw around his neck. The dragon was so big that she could have ripped off Terrence's head without even trying.

Terrence stopped moving. His body slumped, and he shifted back to his human form. The dragon guard that hadn't shifted grabbed his arm. Terrence turned back to Elijah. His eyes were wide, and Donahue was sure he wasn't faking his fear. Maybe he was terrified of the dragon who'd almost eaten him, but something told Donahue that wasn't the case.

"Please," Terrence said again. "I have a family. I need to protect them. I put them in danger by coming here to warn you, but it was the right thing to do. I thought you'd let me go."

Donahue turned to Elijah. It was hard to read the alpha, so Donahue tried to put himself in his place. Even if Elijah believed Terrence's words, his clan was his first priority. He might want to help Terrence and his family, but not before he helped his dragons.

Donahue was glad he wasn't an alpha. He wouldn't have known where to start guiding so many people, and the big decisions Elijah had to make made Donahue want to run away screaming. He'd be a shitty alpha.

"What do you think he'll do to your family?" Elijah asked.

Terrence hesitated as if he wasn't sure he should tell Elijah. He looked around, and Donahue realized they had the attention of what seemed like most of the clan. A bunch of people had gathered around the gate, all of them staring and listening in. If Terrence told Elijah about his family here, the entire clan would know. He might trust Elijah, but the other dragons? Donahue doubted he wanted to give them that kind of ammunition against him.

Terrence's expression sobered. "He'll kill them. If I'm not back by tomorrow morning and he realizes I'm gone, he'll kill them."

Elijah nodded as if he expected that answer. Donahue expected him to tell the guards to let go, but instead, he gestured at them to continue walking. "Take him inside."

Terrence didn't argue again.

Elijah knew what would happen to Terrence's family if Terrence wasn't back tomorrow, but he still decided to have him taken inside. Donahue could only imagine being in Elijah's place, but he hoped the alpha would live up to his reputation. From everything Donahue had heard and been told, Elijah was fair as an alpha and a person. He probably just wanted to ask Terrence some questions and learn more about this coven, and Donahue agreed. If they were going to be attacked by a bunch of mages coming for Valerian, they needed to know who they would face and how powerful they were. The only way to get details was to ask Terrence, but he'd been ready to run, or rather, fly away. Now, he wouldn't be able to.

Donahue grabbed what remained of Terrence's clothes to throw them away. Elijah wouldn't give Terrence his phone back, so Donahue powered it off.

Nothing in this situation felt right, but Donahue didn't make decisions or give orders. If he wanted to continue being a clan member, he had to obey Elijah, even though he worried about the alpha's decisions.

For now, nothing irreparable had been done. There was still a chance that Elijah would let Terrence go in time and that Terrence's alpha wouldn't notice he was gone.

But even if he did notice and took it out on Terrence's

family, technically, it was none of Elijah's business. He was the alpha of a dragon clan, and while he might want to protect anyone who needed it, Terrence was on the side of their enemies right now. If Elijah had to choose, he'd no doubt choose what would give him enough answers to protect his clan, even if it meant the death of people Terrence cherished. It was hard to think about, but Donahue couldn't blame Elijah.

He just hoped things didn't go that far.

CHAPTER FOUR

Terrence had been dragged into the mansion where the dragons lived. He'd been surprised to be taken inside the house, but then he'd realized that he was being taken to the basement.

He looked around. This place was nothing like the house upstairs, but he hadn't expected it to be. It wasn't decorated, and everywhere Terrence looked, he saw cement. There were cement walls and floors, and the space had been divided into smaller cells that were closed with metal doors. There were bars at the small opening in the doors and no windows. The white light was harsh, but there was nothing Terrence could do about it.

Or about anything else.

At least he wasn't too uncomfortable. The cell had a bed and a tiny closed-off area with a toilet. He'd been given a water bottle but hadn't touched it. This place was nicer than anything Irwin would have come up with. Hell, Irwin would have killed Terrence on sight instead of putting him in a cell.

But the fact that Elijah was different from Irwin didn't matter. Elijah was protecting his clan, which Terrence understood, but that meant that Terrence was terrified for his family. He could probably get away with staying out of cockatrice territory for the rest of the day and night, but Irwin would expect him tomorrow morning. It was his turn to see Natasha, and Terrence had never missed a visit. Irwin would instantly understand something was up if Terrence wasn't there, and then all hell would break loose.

Terrence wouldn't be surprised if Irwin hurt his family to get back at him, but he'd probably never find out if he was forced to stay here. He didn't think Elijah wasn't being fair by locking him up. In fact, he understood why the alpha had done it. He just wished things were different.

But they weren't. He'd gotten himself in trouble, and there was no way out. He couldn't break out of the cell, and trying to shift hadn't worked well.

He shouldn't have. If he'd stayed in his human form, he wouldn't have torn off half of his clothes, and he wouldn't be fucking freezing right now.

He wiggled his ass on the mattress he was sitting on and wrapped the blanket he'd found on the bed tighter around his shoulders. What was happening? Elijah had ordered he be taken here, but so far, he hadn't come downstairs to interrogate him. What would happen when he did? Would he torture Terrence? Or would he believe Terrence when he told him everything he wanted to know?

Terrence wasn't planning to keep secrets. He definitely wasn't planning to let the dragons torture him so he could protect the cockatrices. He didn't care if Irwin and his people died. He didn't even care about most of the other cockatrices in his clan. He just cared about his family, and that was who he was afraid for. If he could, he'd hand over Irwin on a silver platter.

Which was what he'd been trying to do, but it hadn't worked out well.

The sound of footsteps coming closer made Terrence tense. He rushed toward the door, ready to beg whoever was there to let him out. He wasn't surprised to see Valerian stop in front of the door. One of the guys from earlier was with him, and when Valerian tried to move closer, the guy grabbed his shoulder and kept him in place.

Who was he? It was clear from the way he touched

Valerian that they were familiar with each other. He was trying to protect Valerian from a cockatrice shifter who could possibly hurt him, and Terrence didn't begrudge him for that.

"How are you?" Valerian asked. "Are you wounded? Is there anything I can do for you?"

"You can tell your alpha that I need to go home."

Valerian tried moving forward again, but the other guy kept him where he was. Valerian glared at him, and the guy glared right back.

"You're not getting any closer to him," the guy said.

"Come on, Cooper. It's Terrence. You know him."

Terrence was surprised to hear that because he didn't think he knew Cooper. He tried to remember, but the only thing he could focus on was going home.

"Cooper's my boyfriend. He was a ghost."

Terrence blinked. He knew about psychics and mages, but it was the first time he'd heard someone say someone else had *been* a ghost. If Cooper was a ghost, Terrence wouldn't be able to see him.

What the fuck was happening?

"Anyway, we're not here to talk about me and Cooper," Valerian said.

Terrence wished he could ask more questions about Cooper, but from the way Cooper was scowling at him, he suspected he wouldn't get answers. That was fine. If Cooper wanted to keep his secrets, he should.

"Why are you here?" Terrence asked. "If it's not to let me go, you might as well leave."

"They're here because Valerian asked to be," Elijah's voice boomed in the hallway outside of Terrence's cell.

Terrence swallowed. He hadn't heard or seen the alpha, and he should have. Elijah had stayed out of sight, but Terrence should have smelled him. Now that he knew Elijah was there, he could, but he'd been so focused on his family and convincing Valerian to let him go that he hadn't before.

Valerian turned to Elijah. "Please give Terrence a chance to explain. If you need more information, ask him. There's no reason to keep him prisoner."

"He's a cockatrice shifter," Elijah pointed out as if Valerian wasn't already aware of who and what Terrence was.

"So? Not all cockatrice shifters are bad, just like not all dragons are good. What matters is the kind of person Terrence is."

"He kept you prisoner," Cooper said.

"He didn't. He's as much a victim of Irwin as I was. He was told to keep an eye on me, and now that he mentioned his family, I know how Irwin forced him to do so. He would have hurt Terrence and his family if Terrence had complained or tried to disobey his orders. I'm sure he got his revenge on Terrence after I ran away. I remember seeing the bruises when Terrence was here with Irwin."

He was right. Curt had been pissed that Valerian was gone, but it had been nothing next to Irwin, who'd been furious that someone had managed to get into their territory. He hadn't done anything to Joe or Natasha, but he'd had both Terrence and his father beaten. Terrence could still feel the pain, even though he'd healed a while ago.

"He helped me, even though he knew he would pay for it if Irwin ever found out," Valerian continued. "He could have hurt me or ignored me and done as little as possible. He could have followed his alpha's orders to the letter, but instead, he gave me food and cared for me when I was hurt. I understand why you don't trust him, but I do."

"Who's to say he won't turn against us because Irwin tells him to?" Cooper asked.

"He might, but if he does, it will be because he's trying to protect his family. Tell me you wouldn't do the same for me or York. Tell me you wouldn't do pretty much anything to keep us safe, including betraying people you know are on the right side."

It didn't look like Cooper would. Terrence still didn't know what to expect from this interrogation, but he'd find out soon enough. He was ready to give Elijah every answer he wanted, but he needed one thing in exchange.

To be allowed to go home and protect his family.

Donahue wished he could be downstairs with Valerian, Cooper, and Elijah. He was curious about Terrence and why he'd done all of this today.

Donahue understood protecting family. He'd do anything to protect his, including killing someone. He wouldn't regret it, either. As long as it meant protecting his parents and his brothers, he would be ruthless.

But why did protecting Terrence's family drive him to come to the dragons to tell them about the coven? It couldn't be nice to live in the cockatrice clan, but as far as Donahue could see, it would have been safer for Terrence to stay there and not say anything. As it was, he was risking a lot to warn the dragons.

Donahue hoped Elijah would keep that in mind. If Terrence was here, offering himself up to his enemies, it had to mean his family was in grave danger from the person who should protect them. Donahue had never thought Irwin was a good alpha, but now he was sure of it. If he were, he would be focusing on making his people happy and keeping them safe, not on pushing them into a war that could be avoided. The dragons wanted nothing more than to be left alone so they could live their lives. The cockatrices were coming at them, and while they would defend themselves, they wouldn't attack first.

Or at least, Donahue didn't think so. He was pretty sure a

lot of people were reaching the end of their patience, and he wasn't far behind. He loathed living like this, always waiting for something to happen. He wanted the war to be over with and the cockatrices to be just a bad memory he didn't have to think about.

"What do you think of that guy?" Olsen asked as he knocked his shoulder against Donahue's.

Donahue was standing at the living room window, but there was nothing to see. Terrence was safely inside, and the guards had gone back to work. Terrence seemed to have come alone, something not everyone had believed.

"I think he's desperate," Donahue said. "I want to listen to that interrogation. I want to find out why he's here and what he wants."

"It's not your business."

"Why not? Elijah didn't tell us to stay away. He didn't tell us anything. He just had Terrence taken downstairs and went there with Valerian and Cooper. Did you ask if you could come along?"

"This isn't a good idea," Olsen warned.

He was probably right. Elijah wouldn't kick Donahue out for this, though. If he didn't want him there, he'd ask him what he wanted, then tell him to fuck off. Donahue could live with that.

He stepped away from the window. Olsen tried to grab his shoulder, but Donahue shrugged off his brother's hand. He wanted answers and didn't see why he shouldn't get them.

"It's your funeral," Olsen warned him.

Donahue winked at him. "Make sure to cry a lot."

Olsen rolled his eyes, but Donahue knew he was worried. He didn't think his brother had any reason to be when it came to Elijah. It wasn't like Donahue was going to visit cockatrice territory. He was just going downstairs in the house he lived in.

He was half surprised that no one tried to stop him, but everyone in the house was distracted. He could hear conversations as he made his way out of the living room and toward the door that led to the basement. He ignored them but kept an ear open in case someone called out to him.

Nothing happened, not even when he opened the door to the basement and snuck through. He closed the door and went down the cement steps, blinking at the brightness of the lights.

The stairs ended in a small room with a table, three chairs, a small couch, and a TV. This place wasn't often used, and it showed. Everything was clean and neat, with no personal objects anywhere.

There was another door, and this one was open. Donahue could see the hallway through it, and Elijah standing with Valerian and Cooper. They weren't far, so it didn't surprise Donahue when Elijah looked up and their eyes met. He waited for the alpha to tell him to go back upstairs, but instead, the corners of Elijah's lips curled up, and he turned back to the conversation he was having with Valerian.

Donahue was careful as he walked closer. Elijah didn't mind him being here. The alpha would have told him if he did.

"Tell me everything again," Elijah ordered, looking into the cell that had to be Terrence's.

Donahue placed himself so that he could see inside. Like he'd thought, Terrence was standing on the other side of the door, looking like he was about to climb out of his skin.

"Irwin killed his cousin because he was threatening to take over the clan. Irwin was pissed when Curt grabbed so many cockatrices and attacked you. It was a bad move, but even after he came home, Curt wasn't deterred. He wanted to attack again and persisted even when Irwin forbade him to do anything. Irwin won't tolerate anyone opposing him, including his family."

Terrence's fingers curled around the bars at the small window. "I'll tell you everything, but you have to let me go."

"We'll see," Elijah said.

Donahue wanted to tell him to say yes. He didn't think Elijah actually wanted to keep Terrence here, although he would understand if the alpha did. They didn't know if they could trust Terrence, even though Valerian did.

But Valerian was the one person here who knew Terrence the best. He'd spent weeks with the cockatrice shifter. They hadn't been friends because they hadn't been allowed to, but that didn't mean they hadn't gotten to know each other. Donahue wanted to trust Valerian and to believe that Terrence was on their side. He looked like he was, and he was saying all the right things.

"After Curt died, we thought Irwin would give up. This fight wasn't his initially, and we all know the dragons are stronger. Instead, he announced that the fight wasn't over. Most people went along with it because it's never good to question Irwin's decisions as an alpha. The few people who tried saying something were silenced."

Donahue wondered if that meant they were killed. It felt like that reaction would be disproportionate, but what did he know? After Curt had attacked the dragons, he wouldn't be surprised by anything. Curt couldn't have actually believed he would win, yet he'd still tried to take over the dragon clan. Maybe it was because he'd been an idiot, or maybe there was something more behind it. Either way, Donahue realized that this wasn't his world, so he should go along with what everyone said and see what happened.

"He's bent on winning this fight, and he was being cautious only because he knew he wouldn't win," Terrence continued. "Then yesterday, a coven visited. I spied on the meeting because I wanted to know what they were doing there, so

I heard what they told Irwin. They said they want Valerian, and Curt had promised to hand him over, but he couldn't do so since he was dead. They don't want anything else. They're ready to help the cockatrices in their fight against the dragons. I guess they know you guys won't ever hand him over just because they ask."

Valerian snorted. "Considering the way they hunted me and my parents, I wouldn't go with them even if I were forced to. I'd rather die."

Cooper didn't look happy at Valerian's choice of words. Donahue understood where both of them were coming from. No one wanted anything to happen to Valerian, and Donahue was sure the dragons would protect him.

"Why did you decide to come to us?" Elijah asked.

"Because life isn't good with Irwin as our alpha. No one likes him, but everyone is terrified. He tends to kill the people who oppose him." Terrence hesitated. "And he has my sister. He's going to force her to marry his son. She's only sixteen and deserves to choose how she wants to live her life. I'm sure you can imagine what will happen to her if Irwin and Eddie have their way. My family and I have been trying to get her out, but we have nowhere to go."

"You came to us."

"Not because I expect you to take us in, although I would be grateful if you did. But we know what will happen to this area if Irwin wins and takes over the region. He hasn't suc ceeded yet because of the humans and you, but it would make everyone's life bleaker if the dragons weren't in the way anymore. Natasha would be forced to marry Eddie and carry his kids, and it's not right. Nothing in this situation is."

Donahue couldn't argue with that.

CHAPTER FIVE

Terrence was still stuck in his cell. He had no idea how much time had passed, but it had been hours. Was it morning already? Had he missed his appointment with his sister? Were his brother and his father worried?

More importantly, had Irwin realized he was gone?

Terrence hadn't seen anyone in hours, so no one could answer his questions. No one could tell him if he'd killed his family by trying to help the dragons. He prayed he hadn't, but if he missed his appointment with his sister, there was a good chance Irwin would know he was up to something. He might not kill them right away, but he'd try to get answers out of them if Terrence didn't go home.

Maybe Irwin would never find out what Terrence had done. He might think Terrence had run away, so he'd probably leave Terrence's family alone. Terrence couldn't help them from where he was, but at least they'd be alive.

But what kind of life would that be for them? What kind of life would it be for Natasha especially?

Terrence stared at the cement ceiling, trying not to think about it. If he did, he got angry, and he didn't know how to deal with that. From the cell, there was nothing he could do to help her. He couldn't stand up to Irwin and make sure his sister wasn't forced to marry Eddie.

Natasha didn't want to be a mother, especially at sixteen. She wanted to finish school and go to college, but Irwin wouldn't allow her to. It was a small miracle that he hadn't forced her to marry his son already, but his patience had limits, and Terrence knew they were reaching it quickly. If he wanted to help Natasha, he'd have to do something soon.

But what could he do from here?

He didn't know. He'd tried explaining why he needed to leave, but it hadn't worked. He wasn't above begging, but the dragons didn't seem to care.

He didn't blame them. Terrence hadn't been there when Curt and the cockatrice shifters he'd gathered had attacked the dragons, but he knew how it had gone. Irwin had lost several cockatrice shifters, and the ones who'd come home had told everyone what had happened in excruciating detail. They'd been wounded and terrified.

Irwin hadn't killed everyone who had participated—just Curt—but he'd punished them. Terrence wondered if he'd had to. After hearing some of the things they'd seen and had lived through, he felt they'd already been punished enough.

But he understood why the dragons were so angry with him, even though he hadn't been there. Curt had attacked them in their home, risking the life of everyone there, especially the most vulnerable of their people like Valerian. He'd killed some of the dragons, like that guard's brother. How could Terrence blame them for not wanting to give him what he needed?

He should have known better. He should have sent them a message or stayed away from the gates. He hadn't chosen to come in. He'd been dragged in and hadn't wanted to fight, but he should have. It wasn't his job to make sure the dragons believed that Irwin had found allies. He'd just needed to let them know, and it would have been enough. Now, he was stuck here.

Footsteps coming down the hallway made him perk up. It was probably someone bringing him food or something like that, but he could try to convince them to let him go. They wouldn't do anything without their alpha's approval, but at least Terrence could say he'd tried. At least they'd brought him some clothes, but that dragon hadn't even looked his way.

He sat up as the door unlocked. He stayed where he was, not wanting whoever was coming in to believe he would attack them. Even if he did, he wouldn't be able to leave the house. He was in the basement, which meant he'd have to climb the stairs and get through the house without being seen. That wasn't going to happen, no matter how fast and quiet he was.

The man entered carrying a tray. Terrence frowned, wondering why the dragons had sent a human to bring him food. His stomach growled at the scent of what had to be breakfast, but he stayed where he was.

The man looked around, clearly wondering where he should put the tray. Eventually, he rolled his eyes and decided to put it down next to Terrence on the bed.

"They could have at least given you a table," he said.

"You speak as if this isn't your clan, too," Terrence told him.

The man blinked. "I guess you're right. I'm not used to being a clan member yet."

"You're new?"

The man took a step back to give Terrence space. Terrence glanced at the tray. The sight of the food made his stomach growl again. Someone had cooked him eggs, bacon, toast, and coffee. He would have felt like a guest if he hadn't been locked in the basement.

"I'm Donahue," the man said. "And yes, I'm new. As are my brothers. We're all psychic, in case you're wondering. Well, all of us except Olsen. He's never been able to see ghosts."

Terrence didn't know what to make of Donahue. Why was this man telling him so many details about his life? It wasn't too private, but telling an enemy so many things still felt odd. "I'm Terrence."

Donahue grinned. "I know. I was there yesterday when you talked to Elijah. You didn't see me, but I was standing in the hallway. I was also there when you first arrived."

Terrence had been able to tell there was someone else, and now that he focused, he recognized Donahue's scent. Why had a human been there? And a new one in the clan, at that? And why had Donahue tried so hard to protect Terrence when he'd been dragged in?

Terrence didn't understand how dragons worked as a clan, but it was none of his business. "I need you to let me go, please. I'm supposed to see my sister today, and if I don't go, the alpha is going to know something's happened. He might not kill my family right away, but he'll be worried that I betrayed him."

Donahue cocked his head. "Why would he think that?"

Terrence glanced at the door. It was still open, and for a moment, he imagined running for it and trying to get out. He knew better than to try. Maybe this was a way to test him and find out what he would do, or maybe Donahue had just forgotten to close the door. Either way, Terrence wouldn't get far. Even if he managed to get to the upper floor, he wasn't getting out of this house unless the dragons allowed him to.

He grabbed a piece of toast and took a bite, wondering if he should answer Donahue's question. He decided he might as well. "Because he knows no one in my family is happy with the way he's doing things. Even more importantly, he knows we don't want Natasha to marry his son. The guy's an asshole."

Donahue grimaced. "That's the impression I got from everything you said yesterday. It's not right that your sister is being forced to marry him, especially if she's as young as you said."

"She's sixteen. She should only be thinking about boyfriends and college, but instead, she has to face the very real possibility that she might soon be a wife, and a mother right after that. It's why I'm here. I have to save her, but I can't do so alone. I have to save my entire family, but there are four of us, and I don't know what to do. I need help."

Terrence set down the piece of toast because it tasted like ash now. He doubted Donahue could do anything for him, but by now, he was ready to beg anyone who came in through the door.

He needed to get out of here.

Donahue understood how Terrence felt. Well, he didn't have a sister who was being forced to marry an asshole, but he understood wanting to protect family. He'd do anything to protect his brothers and his parents, including betraying his alpha.

He really hoped things would never come down to that because he liked Elijah and his life here.

But since he understood Terrence, Terrence's actions made more sense. The dragons were still debating whether or not Irwin had sent Terrence, but Donahue didn't think he had. For one, he doubted that the cockatrice alpha would have the patience to wait for something like this to work. More importantly, he believed Terrence truly wanted to protect his sister. The way he talked about her was too genuine.

Terrence had hoped he could get the dragons to help with his sister, but instead they'd locked him up and kept him prisoner, even though it could mean his family would get hurt.

"I don't have any authority here," he told Terrence. "I'm human and new. I'm just another clan member, and I would never be able to convince Elijah to do or not do something."

Terrence hung his head. "I understand."

Donahue didn't like to see him so defeated, even though they weren't friends. Maybe it was because he could put himself in Terrence's place too easily. "But I don't think you should give up hope. Elijah is a good man and leader, and he listened to what you had to say. He was up half the night talking to people and making decisions."

"But I'm still locked up."

"Hopefully, not for long. He wants to see you once you're done with breakfast."

Terrence's head snapped up. "He wants to see me?"

"Yep. He said to bring you to his office once you're done eating."

Terrence grabbed the piece of toast again and took another bite. "Why isn't he coming downstairs? Why does he want to see me in his office? I'll have to get through the house to do so. That means I'll see more of this place."

Donahue shrugged. "I guess that either he doesn't care, or he trusts you not to use your knowledge against the clan."

Terrence appeared confused. "Why?"

"Well, I'm not in Elijah's brain, but I think that means he believes you. He might even want to help you."

"I'm a cockatrice."

It sounded like Terrence was trying to convince himself this wasn't possible and that Elijah was trying to deceive him. It would make sense, especially since the only alpha Terrence knew was Irwin. Donahue didn't know the guy, but he'd heard enough. Irwin sounded like an asshole who didn't care about his people, which was the opposite of Elijah. Hell, Donahue was pretty sure that Elijah cared about Terrence more than Irwin, and he wasn't even a clan member.

If he could, Elijah would help him. He wouldn't do so if it were detrimental to the dragons, but that didn't mean he'd throw him to the wolves — or, in this case, the cockatrices. Terrence needed all the help he could find, and Elijah would probably offer him that during this meeting.

Donahue was planning to be there. Elijah hadn't told him to leave yesterday, and he'd been the one to ask Donahue to go downstairs to give Terrence food and bring him up to his office. That had to mean something, right?

Maybe it didn't. It didn't make sense for Elijah to allow a human who'd only become a clan member a few weeks ago to be at this meeting. Donahue hadn't tried to be present yesterday when Elijah met with his beta and the other people who helped him with the clan daily. Donahue had known it wasn't his place, but he felt a bit differently about this meeting. Part of him wanted to protect Terrence because he understood why Terrence was doing this. He also wanted to make sure no one hurt Terrence. He'd helped Valerian as much as he could when he'd been a prisoner, and that and the fact that Terrence was so focused on protecting his family told Donahue that he wasn't a bad person. Donahue's opinion didn't matter, but Terrence needed more than Valerian on his side.

It didn't take long for Terrence to finish his breakfast. It had looked like he wouldn't eat earlier, but by the time he was done, his plate was empty, as was his cup of coffee. He used the napkin to clean himself up as well as he could, then got to his feet and grabbed the tray. "We can leave this in the kitchen if I'm allowed to see it."

Elijah hadn't said anything about not showing Terrence some places in the house, so Donahue gestured at him to follow. He left the cell but stayed tense until they reached the upper floor. He didn't like the area downstairs. It was too cold and harsh. The rest of the house was perfect, though, and he grinned when he saw how big Terrence's eyes were as he looked around.

From what Donahue knew, the cockatrices didn't live all in one building the way the dragons did. Valerian had said they all had their own houses, so Terrence probably had never seen so many people living in the same place. It had boggled Donahue's mind initially, too, and it still did sometimes. He enjoyed living surrounded by so many people, though. He liked the feeling of being a part of a massive family.

Donahue ignored the way people were staring as he led the way to the kitchen. It was early morning, so the room was full of people grabbing breakfast. Some of them barely looked awake, while others were ready to head out to work. Everyone watched Terrence put the tray next to the sink and quickly washed his hands. He hesitated, then splashed his face with water.

"I can wash the dishes," he said quietly.

"I'll take care of it," Roslin said, stepping up.

Donahue grinned at his brother. "You just volunteered to fill the dishwasher. What's happened to you?"

"Asshole," Roslin muttered as he bumped against Donahue's shoulder with his to push him out of the way. "Everyone knows you're taking Terrence to Elijah's office. I want you to get there quickly so you can tell me what happened."

"Will do." Donahue looked at Terrence, who was staring at him and Roslin. He gestured at Terrence to follow him again, and the cockatrice shifter did.

"You look close to him," Terrence said.

"I am. It would be weird if I weren't since he's my brother."

"You mentioned you have more than one."

"I have three brothers. Roslin and Victor are psychics, while Olsen is just a regular human being. Victor is the reason we're here. He went and fell in love with a dragon who belongs to this clan."

Donahue could see that Terrence was more relaxed, so he continued talking about his family until they reached the office door. Once they did, Terrence tensed again, and Donahue knew that nothing he could say would help him relax this time.

"I'm sure that everything will be all right," he said as he knocked.

"I hope you're right."

Donahue hoped he was, too.

CHAPTER SIX

Terrence had no idea what to think of any of this. He hadn't expected to be given such a good breakfast or any food at all, and he certainly hadn't expected to be guided through the house to the alpha's office. He didn't know what was happening, and he was terrified, but at the same time, he was hopeful. Surely the alpha wouldn't have asked him to be brought here if he was going to hurt him. He could have done that in the cell, and the clean-up would have been easier.

"Come in," a voice said from inside the room.

Donahue opened the door and stepped into the office without looking back at Terrence. There were no guards around, and it felt like the dragons actually trusted Terrence.

Irwin didn't even trust his own son. He didn't trust anyone, not even other cockatrice shifters from his clan. Seeing an alpha so relaxed around others and not expecting them to try to take him down was odd.

But that was how it felt when Terrence walked into the office. Elijah was still eating breakfast, but he quickly put down his fork and gestured at Terrence to sit in one of the chairs in front of his desk. He didn't tell Donahue to leave, and Terrence wasn't surprised to see that the human decided to stick around and sit in the other chair. He would have, too, if he'd been in his place.

"How are you this morning?" Elijah asked.

He was speaking as if he and Terrence were friends. It was weird. "I'm fine. Confused, mostly."

Elijah nodded. He was a handsome man, much younger

than Irwin. If Terrence had to guess, he had to be in his late thirties, maybe early forties. Irwin was pushing on sixty, and every single year was apparent. Perhaps more than his age, it was because Irwin was always angry, while Elijah was relaxed. The way they lived had to influence the way they looked.

It certainly influenced the way Terrence felt about them. He'd never trusted Irwin, and he disliked his alpha. On the other hand, even though he barely knew Elijah, he liked the man and trusted him more than he did Irwin, even though technically, Elijah was an enemy.

But he'd shown Terrence kindness. Terrence knew what Irwin would have done if he'd been in Elijah's place yesterday. He would have dragged Terrence downstairs and tortured answers out of him. He would have beaten him. There wouldn't have been a bed or a toilet in the cell, and he certainly wouldn't have offered Terrence breakfast.

This was strange, but in the best of ways.

"I'm sorry you had to spend the night in that cell, but I needed to talk to my people. We sent someone into cockatrice territory to check what was happening."

Terrence sucked in a breath. "If Irwin finds them, he'll know something is up."

"Don't worry. We sent ghosts, so unless Curt's girlfriend is around, Irwin won't be able to see them."

"She's still in cockatrice territory, but she's not staying with Irwin." Terrence thought it was a miracle that Irwin hadn't killed her. Maybe he thought he could use her. She'd become a prisoner more than a guest, but Terrence couldn't find it in himself to care.

"That's good to know. Anyway, we have partial confirmation about your situation. Our ghost was able to see your sister and confirm that she lives with Irwin and doesn't seem to want to be there."

Terrence told himself not to hope. He didn't know where Elijah was going with this. "I didn't lie to you. I thought about it, but you're the only person who can help Natasha." Terrence hesitated. He didn't want their family to be separated, but he'd deal with it if that was what it took. "I understand why you don't trust me and don't want me around, but if you could take in at least Natasha, it would be a relief. Me, my brother, and my father can stay with the cockatrices or hide somewhere else. We'll be fine as long as we know Natasha is safe."

"Will you? I doubt Irwin will take it nicely if you take away his son's future wife. He'll see it as a betrayal, and from what I know, those who betray him pay dearly."

They died. There were no two ways about it. If someone betrayed Irwin, they died, and everyone in their clan knew that.

But Terrence was ready to do that and more if it meant saving his family, especially Natasha.

"We'll deal with it when it happens," he murmured.

"How about I make you an offer?"

Terrence perked up, but he was still wary. He wanted to trust Elijah. The alpha hadn't done anything that would cause Terrence not to trust him, and even though Terrence was a prisoner, he'd been treated better than he was treated as a free man with the cockatrices. "What offer?"

"I'm ready to offer you and your family a place within our clan. You'd effectively become clan members, which means you'd be under my protection. You'll be allowed to live here and eventually find work outside of the clan. I believe it would be better to wait until Irwin isn't a problem anymore to do that, though."

Terrence couldn't believe it. What Elijah was offering was what he'd wanted, but it didn't make sense. "We're natural enemies. Dragons and cockatrices have always tried killing each other. Why are you offering this? Especially to three adult men?"

"Because I believe what you told me yesterday. I talked to Valerian and other people and made this decision knowing that you might betray me. But I don't believe you will."

"Of course not. All we've ever wanted was to live our lives in peace. That was never going to be possible if we stayed with the cockatrices. Irwin doesn't want peace. He wants people who will follow his every order and bow to him. He takes and takes, not caring how we feel." He'd taken Natasha to give her to his son. The only reason he hadn't yet was that she was too young, and Irwin had been attempting to save face. That would be over soon.

But maybe Natasha would be all right. Elijah was offering so much more than Terrence had expected, and he could hardly believe it.

"I doubt your people will be happy with that decision," he said, wanting to get all of his doubts all of the way.

"I know some won't be. They don't trust you, and we suffered at the hands of the cockatrices. You will no doubt have to deal with them and defend yourself and your family, but I'll step in if things go too far. I always try to consider how my people will feel about my decisions, but in the end, I'm the alpha. I do what's best for the clan, and right now, I feel that what's best for us is to give you a place to call home." Elijah leaned forward. "I'm doing so because I want to help you, but also because I think you can help us. You lived with the cockatrices all your life, haven't you?"

"I was born there. So were my brother and my sister. My mother died there."

"And you're willing to give us as many details as we need and ask for? If you accept my offer, I need you to truly be a clan member. That means working against the cockatrices."

"I'll give you anything you ask for."

Elijah stared at Terrence for a moment before offering him his hand. "Then I believe we have a deal."

Terrence still had many doubts and questions. He might be leading his family into a different hell, but what choice did he have? It was either this or staying with Irwin, which wasn't possible.

Terrence had two options, and he knew which one he had to take.

He grabbed Elijah's hand and shook it.

Donahue breathed easier now that Terrence had accepted Elijah's offer. It was clear that Terrence wanted a better life for himself and his family, and the easiest way for him to get it was to ally himself with Elijah and the dragons. It didn't sound like he had a lot to betray, anyway. Irwin sounded like an awful alpha, and Terrence had to be happy to leave and find a safe place for his sister and the rest of their family.

"What do you need from me?" Terrence asked as he leaned back in his chair.

"Right now, I need you to behave as if nothing's wrong," Elijah told him. "Donahue is going to drive you back to cockatrice territory. While you're there, we'll put everything together to extract your sister. Your father and brother will be easy, but it's more complicated if she lives with Irwin, like you say."

Terrence's expression was serious. "I think that's why Irwin wanted her there. He's been afraid we'd help Natasha escape after he decided she would marry his son."

Elijah shook his head. He looked as disgusted as Donahue felt. How could anyone force a teenager—barely more than a baby—to get married? Considering everything else Donahue had heard, he wasn't surprised that Terrence was so eager to leave his clan.

"We'll find a way," Elijah assured Terrence. "Don't forget that we have ghosts working with us. They can sneak into Irwin's house without him knowing about them. They'll give us as much information as we need that you can't give us."

"But they can't save my sister."

Elijah smiled. "They won't have to. We will. You and your family are part of our clan, and we take care of our people."

"I still think this is going to bring you more problems than you should have to deal with," Terrence said.

"You leave those problems to me. I'm not the alpha for nothing, and I'm ready to fight for the position if anyone believes they could do a better job. I don't think that will happen, though, especially not so close to a possible war with the cockatrices. You risked a lot to inform us about the coven, and that matters to me. It would have been easier for you to ignore it and continue your life without worrying about us, yet here you are."

"I feel that I have to tell you I'm here because of Natasha," Terrence warned.

Elijah chuckled. "I know. Why you're here doesn't matter. What does is the decision you made, and you decided to help us instead of your clan."

Terrence grinned. "Well, you're my new clan now."

Donahue was excited. He was glad Terrence and his family would be okay, but even more so that this gave them an advantage when it came to the upcoming war. Irwin couldn't know they were aware that he was working with a mage coven, and he wouldn't expect Terrence to betray him. Through Terrence, they could get information they wouldn't have otherwise. It might give them the edge they needed, and if they were lucky, they'd win the war.

But it was only just starting. There was a lot of work to do and not much Donahue could help with. He was only human, and this was a war between shifters.

But the clan was his home, and he wouldn't abandon them in their time of need. He'd do what he could and what Elijah asked him to do.

And since Elijah had asked him to drive Terrence back to cockatrice territory, he would. He wasn't worried. He wouldn't park too close, and if anyone saw him, they'd probably think Terrence had visited with a friend or something. If it came to that, Donahue didn't have a problem with Terrence telling everyone they were dating.

It wasn't hard to imagine.

Terrence was handsome, especially when he was relaxed. Donahue wanted to see him smile and laugh, and since they were now clan members, he knew it would happen eventually. It would be better if this war were over, but Donahue wasn't planning on waiting that long to get to know Terrence. There was no way to know how long it would last and how many people would still be standing at the end, but Donahue prayed he would be one of those people, along with his family and Terrence.

"What do I do, then?" Terrence asked. "I just go on with my life?"

Elijah nodded. "Donahue will give you his number. You can communicate with us through it. He's human and hasn't been a clan member for long, so it shouldn't raise suspicions even if someone notices something. Get through the day as you normally would and warn your family that we'll be extracting them tonight."

Donahue was surprised it would be so soon, and from Terrence's expression, he wasn't the only one.

"Tonight?" Terrence asked.

"It would be best for you not to stay longer. Every day you do means that Irwin has another opportunity to find out you're working against him."

"I'm fine with tonight, and it'll be easy enough for my

brother and my father since we're free to move around, but what about Natasha? She lives with Irwin."

Elijah grinned, but it wasn't a nice smile. It was threatening and toothy, and it made Donahue shiver, even though he knew it wasn't directed at him.

"It's not the first time we've snuck into Irwin's territory and taken someone from him."

"Valerian didn't live with him, though."

"I know you're worried about your sister, and I want you to warn her if you can. It would be easier if she didn't fight us when we reach her. One way or another, though, your family will be free by tomorrow morning."

Terrence looked bewildered. It had to be a lot for him to deal with. When he'd left cockatrice territory yesterday, he'd probably hoped the dragons would welcome him and his family, but if Donahue had been in his place, he wouldn't have been too sure about that.

But Elijah had welcomed Terrence, and his family would soon be safe. After living with Irwin for so long, it had to be odd to think they wouldn't have to be worried for much longer.

"I don't know how to thank you for all of this," Terrence said.

"Help us win the war. Help me protect my clan and my family. That's all I ask of you," Elijah told him.

It was good that Terrence was on their side because even though the dragons were powerful, they'd need all the help they could find to defeat the cockatrices and the mages. Having Terrence was good, but Donahue couldn't help but wonder if it would be enough. The only mage they had was Valerian, and he was still learning how to use his powers. Donahue hoped that others would help, like Gunther and Amelia, but there was no way to be sure, and he couldn't help but worry.

But he had faith in Elijah. The alpha would make all the right decisions. His main goal was to protect the clan and make it out of this war in one piece. Donahue had no doubt they'd lose people, and he hated it, but they'd be victorious in the end.

They had to be.

Terrence wasn't sure he could act as if nothing was happening, but he didn't have a choice. If he wanted to get his family out of cockatrice territory, he'd need to be a better actor than he'd ever been.

It wouldn't be easy, but he'd been hiding his hate for Irwin since he was old enough to start working for the alpha. It had gotten worse after Irwin had forced Natasha to move in with him and his family. Terrence was reaching the end of his rope, but thankfully, things were finally going the way they should.

Elijah had welcomed Terrence and his family into the dragon clan. He'd help Terrence get them out of Irwin's hold. It was everything Terrence had told himself not to hope for, and it was just out of reach. He only needed a bit more patience, and they'd be free and allowed to live their lives the way they wanted.

"I'll do everything I can," Terrence promised.

Elijah nodded. "That's all I ask. I'm sure you need to go, but I'll see you soon. Your family will be here with you by tomorrow morning, but it won't be over yet. We have to win the war."

There was no way to know who would win, especially with the mages working with Irwin, but even though it was scary, Terrence knew he was on the right side. It might not be the winning side, but he couldn't obsess over what would happen if the dragons lost. It was the wrong way to go about this, and he was done being afraid.

He'd been afraid all his life, but soon, he wouldn't have a reason to fear. He'd have a new clan, Irwin and the cockatrices would have lost the war, and everyone would be free to live in peace.

Terrence clung to that as he left Elijah's office. His mind spun with plans and things he needed to do, and the first on his list was to see Natasha. They were never left alone, but they were allowed to hug, which meant Terrence would have a handful of seconds to tell her they were coming to save her. Hopefully, she'd understand and would be ready when the dragons reached her. Terrence wanted to be there when they did, but he didn't know what Elijah was planning and didn't want to be a hindrance. As long as Natasha made it out, he didn't care who rescued her.

He was keenly aware of Donahue walking next to him. The human was talking, but Terrence couldn't focus on what he was saying. Donahue's voice was soothing, though, and Terrence allowed it to pull him out of the swirl of his thoughts and back into the present.

He'd go home, see Natasha, and warn her, then go to his father and brother and do the same. The three of them could pack the things they didn't want to leave behind, and they'd be ready when Elijah and his people came to get them.

Terrence was doing the right thing, and he hoped everyone would agree. Joe might be a problem, but if he had anything to say about them moving in with the dragons, Terrence would talk to him. Joe wanted their family out as much as Terrence did. If he could have, Joe would have used other methods, like facing Irwin head-on. He was young, and he didn't always realize that there was a good reason Irwin was the alpha. He was strong and cruel and never hesitated to hurt people if it meant keeping his control and power.

"My car is outside," Donahue said as he gestured at the front door. "I'll give you my number so you can keep me updated about what's happening with the cockatrices and your family. Hopefully, I won't need to be a liaison for long."

Terrence understood why Donahue felt that way. Donahue was human, and if a fight started between the cockatrices and dragons, it wouldn't be great for him to be in the middle of it. He was putting himself in danger to help Terrence, and Terrence was grateful.

"Thank you for helping me," he said as he followed Donahue toward a car.

Donahue had stopped to pull on a jacket, but Terrence didn't have one. He hadn't thought he'd need it. He'd expected to fly to the dragons, talk to the alpha, then fly back and be at home by last night. Instead, he was still in dragon territory.

Irwin would kill him if he found out.

Between yesterday and this morning, Terrence had given Irwin a long list of reasons to kill him if he ever found out about this. He only had to resist for the rest of the day, though, and he knew he could do it.

He had to.

"You need to stay in the car once we reach cockatrice territory," Terrence said as they climbed into Donahue's car. "There's no reason for you to leave your car, and if you do, it'll get the attention of whoever's watching."

"Won't they wonder who I am?"

Terrence hesitated. He didn't know much about Donahue, but dragons were known to be more accepting than the cockatrices. "They'll probably think I picked you up somewhere yesterday and spent the night with you."

Donahue arched a brow. "And they wouldn't care that you spent the night with a guy?"

"Irwin won't be happy if he believes I did, but even if he finds out, it's only one day."

"The cockatrices aren't as accepting as the dragons?"

Terrence shrugged. He'd grown up with the cockatrices, and while he disliked Irwin and how he guided the clan, he knew that Irwin wasn't the only one with a small mind. "Let's just say that Irwin firmly believes marriage is intended for procreation, not love."

Donahue grimaced. "Not a lot of space for same-sex relationships, then."

"It's one of the reasons I've never had a serious relationship. Irwin looks the other way as long as whatever I do with guys doesn't get serious. I've always known it wouldn't be accepted, so I keep people at arm's length."

"Well, you won't have to do that for much longer. The dragons won't care who you date. My brother's dating one of the male dragons, and they're far from being the only same-sex relationship in the house."

Terrence hadn't thought of himself when he'd decided he needed to pull his family out of the cockatrice clan. He wanted them to be safe and free, and if he could have the same, it would be a nice bonus. It was hard to believe that he could have a relationship and maybe even a family someday.

But first, he and the dragons had work to do. Terrence didn't want to think too much about the future because he was afraid that he might not have one. He'd fight to protect his family and his new clan, but the cockatrices were strong, and with the mages backing them, they'd be even stronger.

But no matter what, Terrence would keep his family safe.

Donahue grew more nervous the closer they got to cockatrice territory. He wouldn't enter it, but he'd still be way too close for him to be comfortable.

He didn't like the thought of sending Terrence back there alone, but they didn't have a choice. As a human, Donahue wouldn't be welcome in cockatrice territory, especially if

Irwin discovered that Donahue and Terrence were together.

Not that they really were. They might not even have to act like they were. It all depended on who was standing guard and who would see them. Just in case, they'd come up with an excuse in case someone saw them together, but Donahue hoped Terrence wouldn't need to use it. They needed to behave as if everything was normal, but Donahue suspected that seeing Terrence with a guy was anything but normal. He might have said that he had one-night stands sometimes, but Donahue couldn't help but wonder how often it happened.

With Irwin being against same-sex relationships, Donahue suspected it wasn't a stretch to think that Terrence tried to avoid being with guys as much as possible, just in case. Donahue might not know Irwin well, but he knew enough to be sure that the alpha would use it against Terrence. He might pull Terrence's sister away from her family, maybe even tell Terrence he couldn't see her anymore.

But even if he did, it wouldn't be for long. Terrence and his family would be safe by the end of the night.

Donahue probably wouldn't have a role in that mission. He was human and wouldn't be able to defeat a cockatrice, let alone an entire clan of them. Elijah wasn't planning on taking the war to them, so it would be better if no one noticed them, but if they did, the dragons could defend themselves.

Donahue, not so much.

"You can park right there," Terrence said as he gestured at the side of the road.

The only thing Donahue could see on that side were trees. He knew the cockatrices lived in the woods and that their houses were hidden from the road. The dragons had a similar setup when it came to privacy, although they'd added a tall fence and a gate. Elijah had bought a massive plot of land and had built the mansion there. He was the first alpha of their clan. He'd created it. Everyone who was there had decided to move in with the clan because they trusted Elijah as their alpha.

Things were different for the cockatrices. Donahue had gotten a crash course on them and their history, so he knew that being an alpha there was passed down from father to son. Irwin's son would become the alpha when his father stepped down or passed away, just like Irwin had become the alpha when his father had done so. Donahue could guess that Irwin's grandfather had been the alpha before then, and so on.

That didn't seem like the best system. Irwin wasn't a good alpha, and the cockatrices should be able to replace him if they felt they couldn't trust him. It was none of Donahue's business, though. Honestly, he didn't care much about the cockatrices. If they truly wanted out, they'd find a way, like Terrence had. It wouldn't be easy, but it was possible.

He parked the car but didn't turn off the engine. He couldn't see anything different in this stretch of road and woods. There were just trees extending as far as he could see.

"How far is your house?"

Terrence gestured in a northwest direction. "Not far that way. Thanks for giving me a ride."

"I would have even if Elijah hadn't told me to," Donahue teased.

Terrence blinked as if he didn't know what to make of that.

Donahue wasn't sure himself. He just knew that he liked Terrence and was excited at the thought of him becoming a clan member. He wanted to get to know Terrence better.

And the only way to do that was to spend time with him.

Terrence suddenly leaned closer. Donahue blinked as he felt Terrence's lips brush against his cheek, then his earlobe. He had no idea what was happening or what to do, so he allowed his instinct to take over. He put his hands on Terrence's forearms but didn't push him away.

"I think someone's watching us," Terrence whispered.

Was it bad that Donahue was disappointed that this might be the only reason Terrence had leaned forward? For a wild moment, Donahue had thought Terrence would kiss him, and he'd been on board. He liked and admired the cockatrice shifter, and he wouldn't mind seeing if there could be something between them.

But first, they needed to get Terrence out of Irwin's claws.

"You should probably go, then," Donahue said.

Terrence nodded and moved back. He quickly got out of the car but leaned back in. "Your number," he whispered.

Donahue held out his hand and quickly entered his number into Terrence's phone when Terrence gave it to him. Once he'd given it back and Terrence was on his way, Donahue waited. He didn't like this, but he couldn't leave until he was sure Terrence was gone. It was stupid, but he sat there in his car and watched as Terrence disappeared. Even the trees were still, and it felt like they were waiting for something to happen.

Donahue was worried about Terrence, but there was nothing he could do there, so he drove away. He'd see Terrence soon.

CHAPTER SEVEN

Terrence tried to act as normal as he could as he walked between the trees. He wasn't sure someone had been watching them, but just in case, he'd acted as if Donahue was just a guy he'd spent the night with. If someone had been there to see it, they wouldn't like it, but it would explain why Donahue had been there and where Terrence had disappeared for the entire night.

But Terrence didn't see or hear anyone as he made his way home. He wasn't late to see Natasha yet and needed a change of clothes since he didn't want to wear the clothes the dragons had given him in case Irwin smelled them on him. He was lucky they'd thought to give him a pair of shoes along with the clothes, because otherwise he'd be walking barefoot.

The house was empty when he reached it, but he wasn't surprised. His brother and father had a shift today, so they were at work. He was supposed to have the night shift, but hopefully he'd be gone by the time he was supposed to start.

He knew he'd have to contribute to the dragon clan's security and was ready to do so. He'd even work nights if he was asked. He wouldn't like it, but he'd know he wouldn't be forced to do it and wouldn't be beaten if something happened while he was on shift. No matter how hard the work might be, it couldn't be harder than working for Irwin.

He tried not to think about what Irwin would do to the people who were on the night shift tonight. When he found out that Natasha and the rest of their family were gone, he'd be pissed and would react accordingly. That usually meant screaming at the people who hadn't done their job, then beating them up so they'd remember to do better next time.

There wouldn't be a next time for Terrence, and he was glad. He didn't want to deal with Irwin anymore. He hoped he would never see him again once he left, but even if he did, they'd be on opposite sides, and the thought made him giddy.

He had time for a shower, so he quickly washed up before dressing again and heading out. He was a little sad at the thought of leaving the house where he'd grown up, and he couldn't wait to see what the future would bring for him and his family. This was the only home he'd ever known, but beyond these walls, he'd never felt like he belonged. Maybe now, he would. At the very least, he wouldn't be afraid something would happen to him or his family. Even if that was the only advantage they got by moving in with dragons, it would give Terrence peace of mind.

Irwin was waiting for Terrence when Terrence reached the house where he lived with his family and kept Natasha prisoner. The alpha scowled when he opened the door. "About time," he snapped.

Terrence checked the time on his phone. "I'm not late."

"You're almost late, and I have better things to do than wait for you."

"I'm sorry."

"Just go see your sister and be quick."

Terrence didn't answer, but Irwin didn't expect him to. He never did.

Terrence had never seen much of the alpha's house. When he visited, he didn't go further than the living room. He didn't *want* to see more of the place, so that was fine with him. He knew which bedroom was Natasha's because she'd told him, so he'd been able to indicate it on a map he'd drawn for Elijah. The dragons would know where to find her.

Like always, the living room was empty when he got there.

He sat down and waited for Natasha, knowing she'd be here soon. He listened to every sound, grinning when he heard footsteps coming down the stairs.

She was in a rush, like always. She despised living here, and Terrence had wished he could take her away many times. Today, finally, he would do it.

But he needed to be careful. He didn't want to tell Natasha too soon in case she said or did something that would catch Irwin's attention. There wasn't usually someone in the room with them when they visited, but Terrence wouldn't put it past Irwin to spy on them. No, it would be better to tell her as he left.

The door swung open, and she appeared. Her long brown hair was in a braid that hung over her left shoulder. She didn't have makeup on, and she wore an oversized sweater that Terrence was pretty sure belonged to Joe, along with a pair of sweatpants. Once, she'd told him that she dressed that way because Eddie didn't like it. They both knew that if they were to ever marry, Eddie would force her to dress the way he wanted, but for now, they were nothing to each other. Natasha took what little freedom she had and wielded it like a weapon, and Terrence loved her for it. He just wished he could have taken his sister away before she ended up in this mess.

She smiled and threw herself into Terrence's arms. He barely managed to get to his feet to catch her, and they held each other tightly for a moment.

"I missed you," Natasha said.

She was only allowed one visit per week, one person at a time. That meant that Terrence, Joe, and their father couldn't come at the same time. They each saw Natasha once every three weeks, and it wasn't enough.

"Tell me what you've been up to since I last saw you," Terrence said as he sat back on the couch and patted the space next to him.

He could have sworn she was different. Every time he saw her, he noticed something he hadn't before. He was in awe every time but also terrified because it meant she was growing up. She wasn't seventeen yet, but her birthday was only a few months away, and Terrence suspected that as soon as it came, Irwin would want her and Eddie to get married.

But they didn't have to think about that anymore because Natasha wouldn't be here to marry Eddie. That made Terrence wonder if Eddie would turn his attention to someone else, but he couldn't afford to worry about the other cockatrice shifters who lived here. None of them had raised a finger to help him and his family, and while he understood why they couldn't, he didn't feel guilty about not being able to help them. In the cockatrice clan, everyone fended for themselves. That was how it always had gone, and Terrence was glad the dragons were different. They worked together for a better life for all of them.

Terrence listened to his sister talk about school and everything else she'd been up to for the past three weeks. She'd have to stay out of school for a bit after they left in case Irwin tried to snatch her from there, but they'd find a way to work with it.

Natasha lightly punched Terrence's shoulder, jerking him out of his thoughts.

"You're distracted," she whispered.

Terrence glanced at the open living room door. They didn't know if Irwin or Eddie might be lurking in the hallway, listening to their conversation. "I'm just tired, and I should go to bed since I have the night shift."

Natasha frowned. "Already? But you just got here."

Terrence wondered how much to tell her. "I was out late last night. I met someone."

"I don't need details. Did you have fun?"

"Yeah, but I didn't get enough sleep. I don't want to cut our visit short, though."

Natasha hugged him. "It's fine. I hate that you worry about me so much."

Since she was in Terrence's arms, he buried his face against her hair, making sure that his lips were close to her ear. He glanced at the door but couldn't hear or see anyone, so he'd have to take the risk.

"You need to be ready tonight. We're getting you out."

Natasha tensed, but thankfully, she didn't do or say anything that would give them up. "How?" she asked.

"I made friends with the dragons." That was all she needed to know. This way, she wouldn't fight the dragons when they got to her.

"I'll see you soon," she said, her voice louder.

They separated, even though Terrence wanted nothing more than to stay here. It wouldn't be for long this time.

He kept that in mind as he made his way to the front door. He was only half surprised to find Eddie lurking in the entrance. The asshole always made a point of needling Terrence when he visited. Terrence was pretty sure he did the same with Joe and their father, but they'd never talked about it. If Eddie did that with Joe, it was a miracle he hadn't gotten a punch to the nose yet.

Terrence nodded at him and opened the door to leave. Eddie cleared his throat, and Terrence tensed, waiting for whatever he had to say. When nothing came, he hurried out of the house, slamming the door shut behind himself.

He didn't breathe easier until he couldn't see the house anymore. Only part of his work for today was done. He'd told Natasha to be ready. Now, it was time to do the same with Joe and their father, but unlike Natasha, they'd have the opportunity to ask questions. Whatever the answers, though, they didn't have a choice. They had to leave.

And they would.

Donahue wasn't surprised when he arrived home and found everyone gathered in the dining room. The table had been transformed from a surface where they ate their meals to a giant desk. Computers were scattered on top of it, along with notepads and too many pens for Donahue to count. Cell phones had been abandoned on the wooden surface, and every chair was occupied.

Donahue hadn't known what to think when Elijah had offered to take in Terrence and his family, but he hadn't expected the alpha to put so much into the rescue. He was impressed, and once again, he knew he'd made the right choice when he'd decided to move here.

"You're back," Olsen said with a smile.

"I am, and this is nothing like what I left this morning. What happened?"

"Everyone's working on setting up tonight's rescue."

"Who's going?"

Olsen grimaced and gestured toward one end of the table. "You'll have to talk to Elijah about that. Valerian already is."

Donahue looked up to find that Valerian was glaring at Elijah. The alpha didn't seem to care, and he was gently talking to Valerian. Donahue wasn't looking forward to entering that debate, but he was curious.

He left his brother behind and headed toward the two. He could tell what the problem was before reaching them, so he wasn't surprised to hear the conversation.

"You'll need a psychic if you want to use Kenneth," Valerian said.

"We do want to use him, and someone will come with us, but not you. We can't afford to put you in that kind of danger," Elijah told him.

"But I know the place. I've been there, so I can tell you where to go."

"Kenneth can do the same. With what we know of Irwin and his alliance with the mages, I'm not willing to take you there. I'm sorry, but you'll have to stay here and wait."

"He's right," Cooper interjected from the chair he was sitting in.

Valerian glared at him, too, but Cooper didn't seem to care. Maybe he was used to having his boyfriend glare at him.

"Think about it," Cooper said. "The mages want you. That's why they offered Irwin an alliance. They can't get you on their own, and it'll be easier to get their hands on you if they use the cockatrices. What will happen if they're there tonight? Do you really want to find out?"

Valerian's expression softened. "I just want to help. Terrence isn't a bad person. I always knew there had to be a good reason for him to follow Irwin and Curt's orders, and I was right. He was protecting his family and his sister."

"And we all know it now. Elijah will ensure that only people on Terrence's side go to get him and his family. I'll even go if it makes you feel better."

That wouldn't be a bad idea. Cooper couldn't shift, but he was dead. When he was wounded, he healed without having to worry about dying. They still didn't know how much his body could take, and Donahue hoped they wouldn't find out tonight, but Cooper would be a great asset.

"You promise you'll be careful?" Valerian asked.

"I will. I might already be dead, but I don't want to be shredded to pieces. I won't be tempting my luck and experimenting."

"I'd like to go, too," Donahue said.

The three turned to him instantly. Valerian huffed, and Donahue knew what he was about to say before he opened his mouth.

"It's not fair," Valerian whined.

Donahue offered him a smile. "You're special. We don't want to risk you, and not just because you're both a psychic and a mage. You're a friend, and the mages are in this fight because they want you. We can't afford for them to snatch you. No one wants me, though. They won't care that I'm there."

"It could be dangerous," Elijah warned.

"I'm aware," Donahue reassured him. "I'll stay back and obey orders. I'm not an idiot. You need help with Kenneth, and I can do that without putting myself in the middle of the fight."

"You're not going anywhere," Donahue's mother snapped from somewhere behind him.

He cringed. He hadn't heard her, but she'd heard him volunteering to put himself in danger.

Donahue didn't want to worry his mother, but he was an adult and wanted to be there for Terrence. They weren't close, but they'd talked, and he thought that Terrence trusted him. He trusted Terrence and believed him when he said he just wanted him and his family to be free and wanted to be there to see it happening. He wanted to help in any way he could.

He faced his mother. "Who's going to go, then? You? Dad?"

"No one from our family is going." She crossed her arms over his chest. "I'm not putting any of you in danger."

"So. what? You'll make Lindsey go? That'll go down well with Jerome."

She grimaced. "He's not trained yet."

"Exactly. I'll be fine."

"It's dangerous."

She was forbidding him to go because she was worried something would happen to him. Donahue understood, but it wouldn't be enough to stop him. "I know, but I'm going anyway."

"I can tie you to your bed."

Donahue laughed. "You could try. It won't change my mind, Mom."

"We'll keep him and everyone else safe," Elijah promised. "We're trying to rescue a young girl from being forced to marry someone she doesn't want. Terrence's sister is only sixteen, and she needs our help."

Elijah knew what he was doing. He'd gotten it right in one, and Donahue saw his mother finally accept this was necessary. She would never leave Natasha in Irwin's hands if there was anything she or someone else could do.

"You'll come home in one piece," she ordered Donahue.

"I promise I will." Donahue had no intention of playing the hero. He also had no intention of fighting with a cockatrice shifter. He'd seen enough of that when they'd attacked, and it would only end up with him bleeding on the floor. "I'll hide behind the closest dragon the entire time. I'm only going so they can understand what Kenneth is saying, and I'm sure he'll keep an eye open so I stay safe. They all will."

Donahue couldn't say he was looking forward to the rescue mission, but he'd been waiting for something to happen, and something finally had. It might only be a small step in the war, but Terrence and his family needed them, and that made it worth it.

When Terrence got home this time, the house wasn't empty. His father and brother were at the kitchen table, their heads close as they quietly talked. Terrence didn't have to ask to know what they were talking about. As soon as he walked in, Joe shot to his feet.

"You're here," he said.

Terrence was exhausted. He hadn't slept well last night in

that cell and wanted nothing more than to throw himself in his bed. Tonight was going to be a mess, and he had to be rested. Everything had to go perfectly so that the dragons could save him and his family.

But first, he'd have to give his family an explanation. They deserved to know what had happened, and even more importantly, they had to be ready when the dragons arrived tonight.

"I'm fine," he promised.

Joe's body was so tense it looked like it might break. They didn't usually fight, especially not physically, but they were all at the end of their ropes. Joe had always been more physical than Terrence, so Terrence wouldn't have been surprised if his brother had tried to hit him. He was frustrated and scared, just like Terrence.

But instead of hitting him, Joe grabbed him by the shoulder and pulled him into his arms. Their hug was short and slightly awkward, and there was a lot of back-patting. Eventually, they separated, and Joe looked more relaxed now.

"I'm sorry. I should have texted you, but I needed to get to Natasha when I returned this morning," Terrence explained as he turned to the coffee pot. He was relieved to see it wasn't empty, so he poured himself a cup. He took a sip, closing his eyes in pleasure.

"You're all right?" his father asked. "What happened with the dragons?"

Terrence sat at the table. He'd already had breakfast, so he wasn't hungry. He was tired and doubted that how long he would sleep today would be enough. He'd been running on fumes for too long and was about to break. He just had to resist a few more hours.

"I'm fine," he told his father. "They didn't hurt me."

"Then why didn't you come back yesterday?" Joe asked.

There was the brother Terrence knew so well.

"The dragons didn't hurt me, but they also weren't happy to see me," Terrence explained. "They dragged me inside and locked me in one of their cells. Luckily, Valerian was there, and the dragon alpha agreed to listen to me. He took his time doing so and talking to his people, which is why he didn't let me go sooner."

"But he did let you go," Terrence's father said.

"He did, and it was with a promise. He and his clan are coming tonight to save us and Natasha. We have to be ready when it happens."

For a moment, the kitchen was completely silent. Terrence gave his family time to wrap their minds around what he'd said. He doubted they'd expected any of this. Terrence had left yesterday to warn the dragons that the cockatrices had allied with a coven. He hadn't expected to become a member of the clan Elijah led, even though he'd hoped they'd somehow help. He hadn't imagined Elijah would take them in, and neither had his family.

"They're doing *what*?" Joe asked.

"You heard me. I didn't expect it, but I had to tell them what was going on with Natasha and Irwin. Elijah wanted to know why I was so eager to return since it was clear that Irwin had never treated me or anyone else the way he should. I begged Elijah to let me go and told him about Natasha, even though I thought it wouldn't change anything. Instead, Elijah showed me what a real alpha's like. He talked to me, asked for details about what's been happening, and agreed to take us in."

"They're rescuing us?" Terrence's father asked as if he couldn't quite believe it.

Terrence nodded. "Tonight. Elijah was grateful that I snuck out to let him know what was happening with the coven. I think that the fact that Valerian has spoken up for me reassured him that it wasn't a trap and that I was doing what I felt was right."

"We can't live with a bunch of dragons," Joe argued.

"I suppose that you don't have to stay if you feel you'd be better off without them," Terrence told him. He didn't have any patience for his brother's temper this morning. "But Natasha and I are going, and I think Dad will, too. We never wanted to be without a clan. We just want to be without the cockatrices and Irwin."

"We can't trust them. They're going to act as if we're part of their clan, then they'll attack us and try to get information out of us about Irwin."

"They don't have to attack us to get information about him. I'll tell them everything they want to know once we're safe." Terrence needed his brother to understand. "Irwin isn't a good alpha. He never was, and he never will be. What he did to Natasha is enough proof of that. You and I both know what will happen if Irwin wins this war. I don't think you want that any more than I do."

"I don't, but how can we trust the dragons?"

"We won't in the beginning. We're natural enemies, and after what Irwin and Curt did to them, I'm stunned they even want to look at us. Elijah is a smart man, though, and he knows that not all cockatrice shifters are bad people. He believes I'm a good person since I warned him about the mages, and he's ready to thank me by letting us stay with them." Terrence looked at their father. "I think it would be for the best, especially for Natasha. There, she'll be able to live her life the way it was supposed to go and make new friends. She can finish high school and go to college without having to worry that she'll have to marry someone she dislikes."

Terrence's father slowly nodded. "How are they going to rescue her? Joe and I are easy because we can just walk out of here, but she can't."

"They're working with a ghost who can go back and forth

without anyone seeing him. He'll go ahead and warn them if there's anyone around. I already told Natasha to be ready when I saw her this morning so she won't freak out when it's time. I'm not entirely sure what the dragons are planning, but they're coming."

"What do they want in exchange for this?" Joe asked. "Because it doesn't matter how good of a man Elijah is. He's still an alpha, and he needs to protect his people. What does he gain from welcoming us into his clan?"

Joe might be young, but he was smart, and Terrence was proud of him. "Information. I don't know much about the coven, but I know a lot about Irwin and his clan. Elijah knows it'll come down to war between us and wants every weapon he can use."

"You want us to betray the cockatrices."

"I want us to make a choice. We wouldn't be running away if it weren't for Irwin. What he's been doing to this clan and our family isn't right, and I'm done with all of it. I don't care if Irwin dies. I don't care if this clan disappears. If anything, it sounds like it would be a good thing. Things are bad enough now, but they'll get worse if Irwin has his way and wins this war. We have to do everything we can to make sure he doesn't, so I'll do what I can, even if it makes me a traitor."

Terrence had already made his decision, and he hoped the rest of his family would follow. He didn't want to leave anyone behind, especially after what would happen tonight.

His father got up and put his cup of coffee in the sink. "I'll start packing," he murmured before exiting the kitchen. Leaving wouldn't be easy for him. This was the house where he'd moved in when he'd gotten married. It was the house where Terrence and his siblings had been born and Terrence's mother had died. It was full of memories.

But the memories weren't linked to the house. They lived in their hearts, and Terrence knew that his father would never forget his mother. No matter what happened or where they lived, she'd always be there to watch over them. She'd want them to save Natasha from a forced marriage.

"You're sure about this?" Joe asked.

"I'm not sure about anything right now except that we need to get Natasha out. Whatever happens next, we'll deal with it." They didn't have a choice.

CHAPTER EIGHT

Donahue couldn't help but wonder what he was doing there. Why had he volunteered for this?

He stared at the dark forest in front of him. He could see lights hidden between the trees, and he wondered how many of the cockatrice shifters were awake. What would happen if they were? Would they attack? Would they even notice that a bunch of dragons had broken into their territory?

Donahue hoped they wouldn't. He had people watching his back, but he'd always lose in a fight against a cockatrice.

"All right?" Cooper asked from Donahue's left.

Donahue nodded even though he wasn't all right. He was nervous and anxious, terrified that someone would see them before they got what they'd come for. He wanted to help Terrence and his family, but he couldn't help but wonder if he and the others were putting themselves in danger by doing so.

They were. They were in cockatrice territory, and if anyone found them, they would be killed. Well, everyone but Cooper, since he was already dead, but Donahue could imagine that would almost be worse. The cockatrices could torture Cooper for a long time, and not just physically. If Cooper had to watch their entire group being killed, he wouldn't come out of it without damage.

Jerome turned toward Cooper and Donahue, and even in the darkness, Donahue could see his glare. He'd been surprised when Jerome had volunteered for this mission. Usually he stuck with his closest family members, even though he was part of the clan. He owed Terrence nothing, yet he was here. Donahue had no idea what to make of it, and now wasn't the right moment to ask.

With Jerome, there would never be a right moment to ask. He'd rather tear off Donahue's head than answer his questions.

Kenneth appeared in front of them, making Donahue jump. He hadn't noticed the ghost, but he should have. What if it had been someone else? Maybe a ghost allied with Irwin? There had to be dead cockatrices around, right?

"Everything looks good at the alpha's house," Kenneth said. "The young woman we're here to rescue is ready to go."

"What about Terrence and his family?"

"Same. Their house isn't far."

Donahue was relieved. He wanted to help Terrence's sister, but he suspected that everyone would be tense if they had to rescue another three people after her. Getting her away from Irwin's house was their plan's most dangerous and delicate part. If anything went wrong, if anyone saw them, they would need to get out of there as soon as possible. That meant they couldn't stop for anyone left behind, including Terrence and the rest of his family.

That was why they went to Terrence's instead of going straight to Irwin's house. Things were a bit more relaxed because they knew where the patrols were, thanks to Terrence. They walked around them, giving them a wide berth, and none of the cockatrice shifters noticed them. Eventually, they reached the house. What would Terrence's family think if they saw them? They were all dressed in black and walking in a line, following a ghost only Donahue could see.

He turned to Kenneth for confirmation that everything was still as it should be. The ghost disappeared inside the house, then quickly came back out through the wall. "Everything's as it should be," he told Donahue. "They're ready, too."

"We should have told them not to bring suitcases," Jerome grumbled.

Donahue wanted to point out that Terrence probably wasn't stupid enough to think they'd be able to drag suitcases through the forest. He liked his head attached to his body, thank you very much.

He quickly knocked on the back door, not one bit surprised when it swung open right away. He and Terrence stared at each other, and Donahue wanted to say something, but there wasn't time.

Jerome pushed Donahue to the side and walked into the house. He looked around, almost as if he expected someone to jump up from behind the furniture and catch them in the act of spiriting the family away.

"Ready?" Donahue asked as he looked at Terrence again.

Terrence nodded. "We are. We didn't overpack, but we did grab what we thought we'd need."

"That's fine as long as you can carry your bags."

"That won't be a problem."

The entire group was in the house now since it was safer here than out in the open.

"Donahue, Cooper, you're with me," Jerome ordered. "The others, take Terrence and his family to the vans."

"I want to come with you," Terrence interjected.

Jerome looked like he was seriously considering eating him. "You shouldn't. You're too close to this. You're going to make a mistake, and then we'll all be in trouble."

"I won't make mistakes. There's nothing I want more than to help my sister, and I won't be able to do that if I'm not careful. I can tell you where to go, though. No one here would be able to do that better than me."

Jerome pinched the bridge of his nose. "Why did I volunteer for this mission again?"

His tone made Donahue smile. "I'm not sure about that,

but it's good to have you with us."

Jerome's expression didn't soften, but he didn't look like he was going to kill someone, which Donahue decided was a good thing.

"I want to come, too," the young man said.

From what Terrence had told Donahue, he had two siblings — Natasha, who they were rescuing from Irwin's house, and Joe. This had to be Joe, so Donahue nodded at him.

Terrence was already shaking his head. "Go with Dad. We'll be there soon."

"It's not fair. I want to help, too."

Donahue wanted to tell Joe that life was unfair, but he didn't need to because Jerome beat him to it.

"Life isn't fair, and when I give an order, you follow it," he snapped. "I'm in charge of this mission. That means you'll obey me, or you'll be left behind. Understood?"

Joe didn't look happy, but he nodded, and with one last glance at Terrence, he followed their father outside. They and most of their group were heading toward the vans they'd parked on the edge of cockatrice territory. Once there, they'd wait for Donahue and the others.

Hopefully, it wouldn't take long, but Donahue didn't fool himself. With his luck, they'd spend the entire night fighting their way back to the vans.

"I'm going to check on the situation again," Kenneth said as he disappeared through the wall.

"Kenneth went to check on what's happening," Donahue informed Jerome.

Jerome nodded, and together, they all waited.

"You shouldn't have come," Terrence told Donahue. "It's dangerous."

"So? Someone needed to be here to talk to Kenneth."

"The ghost?"

Donahue nodded. "Everything's fine. He's been walking

around cockatrice territory since earlier this afternoon. We know where everything is, and we'll get your sister back easily." Or at least, Donahue hoped so.

He understood how important family was and didn't want Terrence's to be torn apart. They just needed to grab Terrence's sister. Everything would be all right.

"We can go," Kenneth said, startling Donahue when he popped back into the kitchen.

Donahue wanted to scold him, but now wasn't the time, so he caught Jerome's eye and nodded. Jerome nodded back and gestured at them to follow him out the door.

They did.

Donahue wasn't the last in line. Cooper was behind him, watching his back, while he looked forward at Kenneth. They didn't have to walk long before Jerome stopped moving, and Donahue knew they'd reached Irwin's house.

Terrence had drawn them a map of the area and of the house, so they knew where to find Natasha. They moved silently around the house, looking for her window. When Terrence found it, he pointed at it, and they stopped.

"What now?" Donahue whispered.

His eyes bugged out when he saw Terrence was stripping. He didn't have to ask why. He'd been living with shifters long enough to know. In a flash, Terrence had shifted and was flying up to the window. He gently bumped the glass with his nose, and the window opened right away.

"Terrence?" a woman asked.

Terrence bobbed his head in a nod. Something was thrown out of the window. Donahue recognized a backpack when it landed. Terrence's sister was prepared, too.

That was when things went sideways.

There wasn't a lot of space, but Terrence managed to hook his talons under Natasha's window. Now that she'd thrown her bag out the window, she needed to get out. Terrence was ready to carry her down, but first, she had to get out of the house.

The bedroom door slammed open. Terrence almost pushed away from the house, but instead, he clung to the side of the window even harder. If he needed to defend his sister, he would.

"I don't have to ask to know who that is," Irwin drawled as he walked inside.

Natasha plastered her back against the wall next to the window. She was close enough that Terrence would be able to drag her out if he had to, but he didn't want to risk hurting her. He'd never forgive himself if something happened to Natasha.

"I knew it was a good idea to ask the mages to put up a silent alarm," Irwin continued as he walked into the room. "Your family hasn't been nice, Natasha. The bunch of you should be thrilled that we chose you to give my son heirs, but instead, you've been ungrateful."

Natasha squared her shoulders. "I'm not ungrateful. I don't want to marry your asshole of a son."

Terrence's eyes widened. Now that Irwin knew they were here, leaving cockatrice territory wouldn't be easy. They had to get out as soon as possible, hopefully before Irwin's guards arrived. That wouldn't happen if Natasha insisted on facing Irwin, so Terrence hoped that she was only distracting him.

He made a soft sound, hoping to get her attention. She slid closer to the window, and Terrence hoped it was because she trusted him to get her to safety. He didn't have a plan, but he was ready to act.

"How dare you?" Irwin bellowed. "You should be grateful that we pulled you out of that dump you call a home. I don't know what my son saw in you, but I told him you weren't the right choice. He could have so much better."

Terrence gaped when Natasha flipped Irwin the bird. She was sixteen, so maybe it wasn't a shock, but Terrence had never seen her like this. She was pissed, and she could finally tell Irwin how she felt about his plans to marry her off to his son.

"*I* can have so much better," she spat out. "And I will."

Terrence had to jerk away from the window when his sister launched herself through it. She shifted before she could fall and hurt herself, opening her wings and screeching as she rose in the air. It had been a long time since she'd been allowed to shift.

The problem was that Irwin was a cockatrice shifter, too. He had wings, which meant he could follow them.

Terrence called out for Natasha and indicated the men waiting for them. Jerome was already shifting, and since the dragon was next to Cooper, Terrence focused on Donahue.

When Terrence flew toward him, Donahue looked terrified, but he didn't move. Terrence didn't know if it was because he thought it was useless or because he was frozen in fear, but it didn't matter.

As soon as he reached Donahue, he grabbed him with his talons. Considering the situation, he was as gentle as he could be, but they couldn't waste any time.

Terrence flew high in the air, keeping above the trees so Donahue wouldn't get hurt. The problem was that it made them more obvious, and within a few seconds, he had two cockatrices hunting him.

Terrence had trained with these people. He might even be able to recognize them by the way they fought. He didn't waste time doing so, though.

He danced out of the way when one of the cockatrices tried to attack him from behind. Talons raked down his back, but he barely felt the pain. He was too focused on trying to get

Donahue out. Natasha was flying next to him, and she screeched in indignation. She started to move toward the cockatrice who'd attacked Terrence, and for a moment, Terrence thought something would happen to her, but a massive dragon intervened before Natasha could reach the cockatrice. Since Cooper was hanging from the dragon's paw, Terrence knew this was Jerome. He opened his mouth, and a column of fire hit the cockatrice.

Terrence's stomach churned at the smell of burnt flesh and at the sound the cockatrice made. He couldn't afford to look back and worry about the cockatrice. He wouldn't like what he might see, anyway.

More cockatrices appeared in the sky. Terrence flew as quickly as he could toward the vans, but he couldn't help but wonder what would happen once they reached them. The cockatrices wouldn't give up. They wanted to defeat Jerome and drag Natasha back to Irwin, and they had their orders. Irwin wouldn't take it nicely if they didn't give him what he'd asked for.

Another dragon appeared in front of Terrence. He flew down, turning a few times to make sure Natasha was following him. He couldn't explain who these dragons were, and he hoped she trusted him enough to know that he'd never put her in any kind of danger if he could avoid it. These dragons were on their side.

The new dragon opened their mouth to fire at the cockatrices. Terrence went down, dropping Donahue once he was sure the human wouldn't get hurt. Donahue yelped and fell to his knees, and while Terrence was worried about him, he was more worried about his sister.

As soon as he touched the ground, he shifted and turned to Natasha. She was right behind him, and when she saw him in his human form, she shifted, too, and threw herself into his arms.

He hugged her tightly, but he didn't dare waste time. He pushed her toward the vans, where everyone else was waiting. Their doors were open, and Terrence could see his father and his brother already climbing out of the closest one.

He pushed Natasha toward it. She ran to the rest of their family, hugging them and crying.

"This is hers," someone said, startling Terrence.

He turned to see Cooper holding out a backpack. He'd been surprised to see the man earlier and wanted to ask why Cooper was there, since it was obvious he didn't like him. He suspected his presence here had to do with Valerian, though, and that was a touchy subject.

"Thank you."

Terrence went to the van and handed the bag to his sister. He grabbed clothes from Joe and quickly dressed as he watched the fight in the air. There were too many cockatrices for the dragons to win, but they were still doing a lot of damage. It would take some time for Irwin to get his people healed and ready to go after tonight.

They weren't supposed to be discovered, but they had been. Hopefully it would end up being an advantage for them rather than putting them in more danger than they were already in.

Jerome landed and shifted. "Everyone, get in the vans. We're leaving now."

Terrence obeyed. He wanted to know what was happening, but he wasn't in charge of this operation. He climbed into the van where his family already was, and Natasha wrapped her arms around him. He sat down, holding her close and burying his nose against her hair. For so long, he hadn't thought he would get this again. He'd believed she was too far out of his reach and that she'd never be part of their family again.

But she was here, and she wasn't the only one. Donahue

had chosen this van, too, and he was sitting close by, doing his best not to stare. He was human, so it had to be odd for him to see these half-naked people hugging each other.

"I'm sorry I grabbed you the way I did," Terrence told him.

Donahue snorted. "I'm pretty sure I'd be cockatrice food if you hadn't, so don't worry about it." He paused and cocked his head. "What do cockatrice shifters eat, anyway?"

Terrence relaxed in his seat. They'd done it.

Well, almost. They still weren't safe. They had to reach the house first, and it wouldn't be easy. He was sure they could do it, though.

He wouldn't have it any other way when he was so close to finally having his family completely free from Irwin.

Donahue had never really thought about how scary it was to fly. He'd taken airplanes, but flying in the clutches of a cockatrice shifter had been terrifying.

Donahue hadn't expected Terrence to drop him, but he'd still felt like he was about to splatter on the ground at any second. The fact that cockatrice shifters were attacking them hadn't helped. Donahue had been sure he wouldn't survive the night, and he'd thought about his mother and how she'd forbidden him to come.

But he was all right and in one piece. Terrence had even apologized for grabbing him the way he had, even though there hadn't been another way to do this. It was the only way for them to be safe as quickly as possible, and it had worked. They were in the vans, headed toward home.

With a bunch of cockatrice shifters flying after them.

He leaned forward, trying to peek out the windows, but it was dark, and he couldn't see anything. "You think they're going to follow us to the house?" he asked no one in particular.

"Irwin is stubborn enough to order it," Terrence's sister said.

Donahue smiled at her. "Hi there. I'm Donahue, one of your brother's friends."

"You're not a shifter."

"I'm a psychic and fully human."

"You live with the dragons?"

"I do, and so do you now."

"As long as I never have to see Eddie again, I don't care where I live."

Donahue could only imagine what she'd been through. Having to fear being forced to marry someone she despised, especially at her age, couldn't have been easy.

But she was free now and wouldn't have to marry anyone she disliked. Terrence and the rest of the family wouldn't have to work for Irwin ever again, and they could see each other anytime they wanted.

Things would be tense for a little while, but Donahue was convinced that eventually, everyone would realize that Elijah had done the only thing he could have done. Terrence had needed help, and he'd offered information in exchange. Elijah would've been a fool not to accept his offer and a cruel man if he'd refused to help Natasha.

The silence in the van was tense as they drove through the metro area. Cockatrice territory was on the opposite side of the city, so it took them a while. Donahue wanted to ask about the cockatrices following them again, but he wasn't sure he wanted to find out if they were still flying above them, waiting for the perfect moment to attack.

The van eventually passed through the gates and parked in front of the house, and it was time for them to get out. Were they about to be attacked?

"They stopped following us a while ago when we entered downtown," Cooper said as he twisted in the front seat. "I don't think they'll follow us here, even though they know where we are. It should be fine to leave the van."

"There's no way to be sure?"

"Open the door and check."

Donahue glared, but Cooper was right. There was only one way to find out.

He opened the door and peeked outside. The front of the house was illuminated, and as he watched, the door flew open. He cringed when he saw that his mother was the first one out, because he didn't want her to be snatched up if the cockatrices had followed.

Nothing happened, so Donahue breathed easier — until his mother grabbed him and dragged him out of the van. He sputtered, but she was already hugging him.

"Don't ever do that to me again," she said. "I forbid you to put yourself in danger like that."

"I'm fine," he reassured her.

"I don't care. I was terrified the entire time. I'm not losing any of my sons."

She turned her attention to the rest of the group. She nodded at Terrence and his family, but her focus was on Natasha.

"How are you?" she asked her. "I'm Donahue's mother, Evangeline. Let me show you to your room."

Natasha turned wide eyes to Terrence, who nodded without hesitation. It felt good to see that he trusted Donahue's family.

Terrence's father and his brother stayed outside for a moment longer. Everyone was watching the sky, but nothing happened. It looked like the cockatrices had stopped following them and wouldn't attack, which was a relief.

But they weren't out of the woods yet. The war had only just started, and now Irwin was pissed. He'd want revenge and wouldn't hesitate to use the coven to get it. Irwin didn't care how many people he hurt. In fact, Donahue suspected that the more people he hurt, the better he felt. To him, the dragons deserved to die.

And he wanted to be the one to kill them.

Terrence knew he should go with his sister, but he was terrified that Irwin had followed them. He couldn't seem to move from the area outside the house, where he was still staring at the sky.

"Gentlemen, it's good to see you," a voice said.

Terrence turned and found Elijah coming toward him. He hadn't noticed him leaving the house, but from their expression, his brother and his father had. Joe looked like he was about to start a fight, while Terrence's father appeared wary. Terrence hoped Joe wouldn't say or do anything to get them kicked out of the clan before they could settle in.

"It's good to be here," he told Elijah. "This is my father, Ronan, and my brother, Joe."

Elijah inclined his head at them but didn't move closer or offer them his hand. It was a smart decision. They weren't afraid, but they didn't trust Elijah. In time, that would change.

Hopefully.

"Jerome told me that the rescue was eventful," Elijah said. "It doesn't look like the cockatrices followed you here, but we're keeping an eye out. You should come inside and meet the rest of the clan."

"Are you sure the cockatrices won't come all the way here?" Terrence asked.

"They would have had to fly over or around the city. Of course, they know where we are, but I don't think Irwin wants to draw the attention of the nearby humans. We already had enough of that recently, and not all of it was good for him."

Terrence remembered that he'd read an article that reflected the truth more than any others. It seemed like the humans in the city didn't care who they trashed when it came to shifters, but this particular journalist had told the truth. He'd explained that the cockatrices had attacked the dragons, and Terrence had been surprised that no one had contacted Irwin to discuss it. The humans were probably afraid, and as long as the dragons and the cockatrices kept the fight in their territories, they'd stay out of it. It was a smart decision, but if Irwin won, it wouldn't help them.

"I don't understand why you want us here," Joe blurted out.

Terrence groaned. He glared at his brother, but Joe didn't notice. He was staring at Elijah as he waited for his answer.

Luckily, Elijah didn't seem offended. He smiled and gestured at the house. "We can talk about it, but we should head inside. Even if the cockatrices didn't follow you, there's always a chance Irwin will do something stupid."

Joe snorted. "He always does something stupid."

"I see we have the same opinion of him."

For some reason, that seemed to mollify Joe. He nodded and stepped closer to the alpha, hesitantly offering his hand. Terrence had a hard time believing it. He'd thought his brother would brood and mope. Joe hadn't wanted to come here. He wanted them to move away entirely, and Terrence had considered it, but they needed protection, especially Natasha. Irwin might not be as powerful away from the city as he was here, but there was still a chance he might be able to find them or get Natasha, and Terrence couldn't allow that to happen. Staying with the dragons was the smartest thing for their family, and it was a relief to see that Joe understood.

"Thank you for taking us in," Joe said.

Elijah shook his hand. "It's the least I can do, since your brother agreed to give me information about the cockatrices and Irwin. Besides, after he told me about your sister, I couldn't leave her there without protection. What Irwin and his son were planning to do is horrible."

"And that's just the tip of the iceberg. They're awful people."

Elijah nodded and gestured at Joe, Terrence, and Ronan to follow him. There were still a few dragons hanging around the vans. They'd piled the bags they'd found in the vans by the stone steps that led to the front door, so Terrence grabbed his and Natasha's. He followed Elijah inside, and even though he'd been here yesterday, he couldn't help but look around.

The place was massive. It had to be, to house an entire dragon clan. Terrence was used to living with people, but not so closely. Back in cockatrice territory, every family had their own home. They didn't live on top of each other like the dragons did, and it would take some time to get used to. As long as they were safe and had food in their stomachs and a roof over their heads, though, he didn't care how long it took.

"Dinner is almost ready," Elijah said. "We waited until you got here, so it's a bit late, but we usually eat around seven PM. You're welcome to visit the kitchen and eat whenever you want. Donahue's mother has already taken Natasha upstairs. Someone will take the three of you and show you to your rooms. I chose rooms close to each other so you can be together."

Terrence wondered if someone had needed to move out to give them space, but he didn't want to know the answer to that question. Convincing some of the dragons that having them here was a good idea would be hard enough. He hoped he hadn't taken the home of any of them.

"I'll show you," Donahue volunteered.

He'd been hanging by the living room door, talking to another man. Terrence wanted to ask who the guy was, but instead, he nodded. "Donahue, this is my father and my brother."

Donahue smiled. "It's a pleasure to meet you."

They hadn't introduced themselves in the van. Things had been too frantic, even as they'd been on the road to come here. Everyone had been terrified of what the cockatrices would do, so there hadn't been a chance to relax.

Now they could, and Terrence could feel his legs start to shake. The adrenaline was leaving his body, and he needed to sit down, take a deep breath, and allow himself to truly believe he was safe.

Joe and Ronan stared around with wide eyes as Donahue led them upstairs. Terrence was too tired to really care about the place. He'd already seen how luxurious it was, so he wasn't surprised that the upstairs reflected what he'd seen downstairs. He knew that tomorrow, it would hit him that he truly lived here now, but at the moment, he wanted nothing more than food, shower, and sleep.

"Your sister is in there," Donahue said as he pointed to an open door.

Terrence could hear voices coming from inside. He wanted to check in on Natasha, but she sounded like she was having fun. She even laughed, a sound Terrence hadn't heard in too long. From what he could hear, Donahue's mother was with her, and even though he didn't know the woman, he felt he could trust her. Besides, Natasha had shown that she could defend herself today. She hadn't hesitated to throw herself out the window to escape Irwin, and she'd wanted to defend Terrence when he'd been attacked.

Terrence rolled his shoulders. It was a bit painful, but he'd heal in no time. He'd ask his father to check the wounds once he was showered.

Donahue eyed Terrence as if he could read his mind. Terrence was surprised he hadn't asked him about the wounds yet, but maybe he didn't remember, or maybe he didn't realize that something had happened while they'd been flying. He'd probably been focused on what was happening to him rather than Terrence.

"These three rooms are yours," Donahue said, opening three more doors. "You can choose which one you'd rather have. They're similar, although they face two different sides of the house."

Terrence waited until his father and brother had chosen a room to step into the last one. He didn't really care where he ended up, but he liked that the room was comfortable. It was bigger than the bedroom he had at home.

The bed was king-sized and had been placed next to a wide window that made it possible to see the stars from the bed. There was a dresser, a closet, two nightstands, and a small sitting area with a coffee table and a couch. There seemed to be a balcony, but Terrence could wait to explore it. The door next to the bed had to lead to the bathroom, and his skin itched for him to take a shower.

"I'll give you time to settle in," Donahue said gently. "Dinner should be ready in about half an hour. Just go downstairs, and I'll meet you in the entrance." He hesitated. For a moment, Terrence wondered what he was thinking. He didn't have to wait long. To his surprise, Donahue stepped closer and pressed a hand against Terrence's chest. Terrence opened his mouth to ask what he was doing, but Donahue was still moving. He pressed their lips together, stunning Terrence into silence.

The kiss was quick, but it was a kiss. When Donahue moved back, he was smiling, and Terrence found himself mirroring the expression. That made Donahue smile even wider, and he patted Terrence's chest.

"I'll see you soon," he promised.

Terrence hadn't expected things to go this well once they moved in with the dragons, but how could he regret his decision when his family was safe and Donahue had kissed him?

CHAPTER NINE

Terrence and his family had been with the dragons for two days, and to his surprise, everything was going well.

Irwin had always said that the dragons were cruel and would kill the cockatrices to take their territory, and while Terrence had known that wasn't true, he hadn't expected them to welcome him and his family with open arms the way they had.

It was overwhelming. Terrence had spent most of yesterday sleeping and recuperating. Eventually, he wanted to talk to Elijah and tell him what he knew about Irwin and ask for a job, but for the moment, he was happy to relax and spend time with his family. They'd been afraid and tense for so long that it felt odd not to worry about Natasha or be scared that something would happen to one of them.

They'd been spending as much time together as they could. Not having to beg to see Natasha felt good, and she seemed to be having the time of her life. She'd been spending a lot of time with Donahue's mother, maybe because she'd been missing that kind of presence in her life. Their mother had died when Natasha was a little girl, and while Terrence, his brother, and their father had done what they could to raise her, it had been a decidedly masculine home. Here, Natasha had plenty of women to spend time with, and she was taking advantage of that. She was already making friends, and it was good to see after she'd been locked up for so long.

A year felt like an eternity at her age, and Terrence had feared how much she would have changed when it was over.

She seemed to be taking to living with the dragons easily, though, and that was all Terrence wanted. It was as if Natasha had always been part of the dragon clan, but things were a bit different when it came to Terrence.

He hadn't been keeping to himself on purpose, but he was focused on sleeping, resting, and spending time with his family. His brother was still a little wary of the dragons, but he'd relaxed. As for their father, he'd taken to living here like a fish in water. Every time Terrence saw him, he was talking to someone new.

Even now that they were at lunch, Terrence's father was sitting between two dragons. He was animatedly talking to the man, but Terrence didn't miss the way he was keeping an eye on the woman on his other side. For some reason, he kept asking her if she wanted more to drink or eat. When Terrence looked closer, hoping no one would notice, he realized the woman had recently been wounded. There were scars on her skin, and sometimes, she appeared a little shaky. It explained why his father was focused on her.

Terrence glanced around the table. Even though he and his family shouldn't fit here, they'd blended in so seamlessly that they looked like they belonged. Terrence's father was talking with his new friends, and while Joe was quiet, Terrence noticed one of Donahue's brothers had pulled him into a conversation. Natasha was chatting with Donahue's mother and a girl about her age, gesturing as she did so.

Then there was Terrence. He wasn't isolating himself, but he found it a bit harder to let go. He'd always been awkward when it came to making friends, maybe because he hadn't wanted to be friends with the other cockatrices. He'd worked and had kept his family safe. It hadn't left a lot of space for friends, especially when he didn't know who he could trust.

Here, he was pretty sure he could trust everyone, but he still found it awkward to go up to someone and start talking to them. He doubted anyone would be offended if he did, but he was fine being on his own for now.

He should have known it wouldn't be for long. The chair next to him slid away from the table, and he looked up to find Donahue. He was carrying a plate and smiling as if this was something he'd done all his life.

"I didn't see you this morning," Donahue said.

"I slept in," Terrence admitted, feeling sheepish.

But Donahue didn't judge him for it. "You earned it," he said as he started eating.

Terrence didn't feel like he'd earned much. The only thing he'd done was save his family, and he still couldn't believe he'd found himself in this situation because of that. "I don't know."

"You did. You spent your life walking on eggshells because you were afraid of what Irwin would do. Especially after he took your sister, you were hypervigilant. It's normal that now that you have the space to relax, your body is recuperating. Don't blame yourself for it."

"I don't."

But Terrence still felt guilty. He needed to do more so that the dragons wouldn't regret letting him and his family in. Maybe he could visit Elijah this afternoon and tell him more about Irwin and the cockatrices. The problem was that there wasn't much he could say that he hadn't already. Elijah needed recent information, not to know how much of an asshole Irwin was.

Donahue knocked their shoulders together. "Relax," he said with a smile. "I know it's not that easy, but you *can* relax now that you're here. The dragons have your back, and so do I."

Terrence found himself smiling. The dragons did have his back, and they'd protect him and his family from Irwin and the cockatrices. Terrence didn't have to be on edge anymore.

And since he didn't have to be as careful as before, maybe it was time for him to explore everything he'd been missing because of Irwin, including relationships.

Donahue could see that Terrence didn't feel at home yet and wasn't surprised. It had taken him a while to feel like he belonged with the dragons, and he didn't have Terrence's history with them. He was human and had moved in with the dragons after his brother had become a clan member. In a way, he did belong.

But not Terrence. He was a cockatrice shifter, an enemy of the dragons. Donahue didn't fully understand why dragons and cockatrices felt like enemies, but he wasn't sure he *could* understand, since he was human. They'd fought for hundreds of years, never allowing themselves to get to know each other and see that they were more similar than they thought.

He was pretty sure someone would beat him up if he dared say that out loud.

Some of the dragons were still hesitant and wary when it came to Terrence and his family. That was understandable, too, so Donahue had done his best to make Terrence feel like he was home. He didn't feel the same sense of having to protect his territory as some of the dragons did, and since Terrence already knew Donahue, Donahue had figured he'd be the best person to do so.

The kiss had something to do with it, too. Donahue still wasn't sure what had possessed him to kiss Terrence, but he had, and he didn't regret it. He liked Terrence, and now that Terrence was here and safe, maybe it was time to see what could happen between them. Donahue didn't want to push too hard or fast, though, so he'd been giving Terrence all the time and space he needed. Terrence knew Donahue liked him. He could be the one to take the next step when he was ready to do so.

"I know the people here have my back," Terrence murmured as he looked around the table. "I just don't feel like I belong yet."

"You will in time."

It reminded Donahue of his position with the clan. He and his family had moved here because it had been safer, but Elijah had never told them they were clan members. They behaved like they were, and no one had ever said they didn't belong, but what would happen when the mess with the cockatrices was over? Would they still belong? They weren't shifters, after all. Victor wouldn't be going anywhere, but that was because he was dating one of the dragons. Donahue was pretty sure that Jerome and his friend Will would move out as soon as they could, although maybe Will would stick around since his boyfriend had lived here before meeting him.

But what about Donahue and his brothers? What about their parents? Donahue doubted Elijah would kick them out, but it would make him feel better if he could talk to the alpha and ask him about it. Elijah would have time for him if he mentioned it, but it wasn't the right moment to do so. Elijah was focused on the cockatrices and what they were doing, and Donahue felt stupid at the thought of bringing up his doubts about sticking around once the war was over.

Besides, what would happen when it was over? Who would win? Even if dragons did — and Donahue prayed they did — they would lose people. They would need time to get back to some kind of normalcy, and that wouldn't be the right moment for Donahue to ask if he could stay forever, either. Maybe he should talk to Elijah sooner rather than later.

He was still thinking about it after lunch. He wanted to stay with Terrence, but the shifter made a beeline for his father, so Donahue let him be. He didn't want to go outside because it was too cold, so he found himself wandering around the house until he reached the library. He peeked inside to make sure there wasn't a lesson going on, and since the room was empty, he walked in.

He'd *thought* the room was empty, but he found his brother Olsen tucked into an armchair, reading a book. He looked up when he heard Donahue.

"And here I thought I could have some privacy and a quiet space."

Donahue gestured at the door. "I can leave."

Olsen closed his book and shook his head. "You don't have to. I'd rather you stay and tell me what's making you all sad and mopey."

"Sad and mopey?"

Olsen pointed at Donahue's face. "You know what I'm talking about. Why do you look like a dragon stole your puppy?"

Donahue settled into another armchair. "I was just thinking about what would happen once the war ended. Do we belong with the dragons?"

"I don't know if we belong, but I know I'm never leaving this place."

Donahue blinked. "You're not?"

"Why would I?"

"I know you had to give up your apartment, but you had a life in the city before moving in with the dragons."

"I can still have a life in the city, even though I moved. I had to quit my job since Elijah thought it would be safer, and it gave me time to think about what I want to do. I've already talked to him, and he agrees I can stay. I like the sense of community here, even though I'm human and nothing special." Olsen smiled deprecatingly. "I'll always be human and not special, but I'm used to it. Feeling it here instead of in the city doesn't change anything."

"Don't say that."

Donahue hated that his brother felt like that. No one could do anything about the fact that Olsen was the only non-psychic in a psychic family. They'd always tried not to make him feel like he didn't belong, but it wasn't always easy for him. He couldn't put himself in his brother's place, but he could imagine how much it hurt.

Olsen waved Donahue's words away. "I'm not offended. It's a fact that I'm not a psychic and never will be. I've made my peace with it, and I'm glad I found a place to call home."

"You didn't feel like you had a home before?" It hurt and made Donahue wonder what else he could have done for Olsen.

"Of course I had a home with you and the rest of the family. I'm talking about the rest of my life. I always felt like I didn't quite fit, but here I feel like I do, even though I really don't. I don't want to go back to an empty apartment. I like living here, and I'll continue doing so."

"You're sure I've never made you feel like you don't belong?"

Olsen rolled his eyes. "We're fine." He grinned. "I think you should focus more on your new boyfriend."

Unfortunately, Donahue didn't have anything to throw at his brother's head. "I don't have a boyfriend."

"*Yet*, but I don't think Terrence will need a lot of convincing to date you. I saw the way you two look at each other."

Donahue smiled at his brother. Everything was a mess right now with the cockatrices and the threat of war on the horizon, but even then, Donahue was happy. His family was safe, he enjoyed living here, and now, he had Terrence.

Maybe. They'd have to talk, but Donahue was hopeful. He was pretty sure Terrence liked him. The one thing they needed to do was talk and find out if they both wanted the same thing.

Donahue was pretty sure they did.

CHAPTER TEN

Irwin had been calling Terrence since he and his family had left cockatrice territory. Terrence had been stunned to see the name on his phone the first time, but he hadn't answered. He suspected that Irwin just wanted to yell at him, and he'd had enough of that while living with the cockatrices.

But Irwin was worse than a scorned ex. He kept calling, even though Terrence never answered. Terrence didn't dare block his number, just in case. He suspected Irwin would find a way around it, and Terrence would rather know Irwin was calling than answer a phone call from a number he didn't know and find out it was him.

"Ignore him," Donahue said.

They were in the kitchen, helping with dinner. Terrence hadn't realized how much work it was, but he should have. With so many dragons living here, they had to cook a massive amount of food every night. Even when not everyone ate dinner, the fridges were full of leftovers.

Donahue seemed to know what he was doing. Terrence was a bit more hesitant, which explained why Donahue had assigned him the vegetables. As long as Donahue told him how much stuff to cut, Terrence was glad to help.

He'd placed his phone on the counter, which was how Donahue had seen who was calling. Terrence had explained his reasoning for not blocking Irwin's number when Donahue had asked, but he was tempted to say fuck it and block Irwin.

He'd already called five times in the past half hour. This was the sixth, and resisting the urge to throw the phone at the wall was almost impossible.

"How can I ignore him?" Terrence asked Donahue. He didn't expect an answer, but he was frustrated. He'd thought he'd left all of that behind and that he'd never have to deal with Irwin again, yet here he was.

"Easy. Just don't look at the phone," Donahue teased. "If you want, I can distract you."

Terrence's body flushed. He did want Donahue to distract him. He wasn't sure how to ask for it, but Donahue didn't seem to have the same problem. He was pretty straightforward when he wanted something. They hadn't talked yet, but Terrence had noticed how Donahue kept touching him when they spent time together. It was nothing as bold as the kiss, but Donahue was still driving him up the wall.

Except that right now, he wasn't the only one. Terrence's phone started vibrating again only seconds after it stopped, Irwin's name flashing on the screen. Terrence had enough. He snatched up the phone, ignored Donahue, and answered. "What?"

There was a moment of silence, as if Irwin couldn't believe Terrence had answered. He probably couldn't since Terrence had been ignoring him for days.

"Is that the way to talk to your alpha?" Irwin eventually asked.

He had always been a pompous asshole, but for some reason, it didn't scare Terrence anymore. He could laugh about it now that he wasn't with the cockatrices anymore. "It's not the way I answer when Elijah calls. You're not my alpha anymore, so I'll answer however I want. You need to stop calling me. I don't know why you are, but no one from my family is coming back. Natasha certainly isn't. I won't allow you to force her to marry that asshole you call a son."

"How dare you?" Irwin asked with a growl.

"No, how dare *you* call me? I don't want anything to do

115

with you. We should have left a long time ago, but we were too afraid and didn't have a place to go. Now, we do, and we're happy."

"You won't be when I go to the press."

Terrence blinked as he tried to understand what Irwin was saying. "To tell them what?"

"That the dragons kidnapped you and your family. They took away four productive members of my clan, including my son's fiancé. How do you think that'll go down?"

Terrence's stomach churned. He was scared of what people's reaction would be if Irwin went to the press, but it also made him angry. How dare Irwin threaten him like that? Did he think it was going to work?

To be honest, it might have if Natasha hadn't been involved. If it had been only Terrence, or maybe even only him and his brother and father, he might have listened, but there was no way he was putting Natasha back in Irwin's hands. Just for her, Terrence would stay away from Irwin, no matter the consequences.

"I won't allow you to control my life or my family anymore," Terrence snapped. "If you go to the press, I'll do the same. I'll tell them how you treat your clan members and what you were trying to do to my sister. I don't think people will like it much when they find out that you attempted to force a sixteen-year-old girl to marry your adult son. I'll also make sure to tell them that you're planning to attack the dragon clan. Curt already did, and you saw how that went down. Do you want to try it a second time?"

"Curt was a fool," Irwin growled.

"And you're an idiot. Calling me is useless. We're never coming back, no matter what you threaten us with. Just let us go, Irwin. You won't gain anything by pulling us back into the clan, and we have people who will fight for us if you try."

"They'll betray you eventually. They're dragons."

"If they do, we'll deal with it. Right now, we're happier than we ever were when we were with the clan, and I don't see that changing. The best thing you can do is let it go. Leave the dragons alone. Leave me and my family alone. We don't want anything from you. You're the one doing all of this, and it's going to be a mess if you continue."

Terrence hung up without giving Irwin time to argue. He didn't think Irwin would listen and give up this war. He wanted what the dragons had, even though it wasn't his to take. That was what Irwin did, though, just like he had with Natasha.

Donahue squeezed Terrence's shoulder and kissed his cheek. "You did good. You're strong, and you stood up to him."

"He threatened to go to the press. He wants to tell them that Elijah kidnapped me and my family."

Donahue's eyes widened. "I doubt anyone would believe that. Even if they do, they'll know it's a lie as soon as they talk to you."

"What if they don't talk to us? What if they believe what Irwin is saying?"

"Elijah has a journalist friend. We'll be fine."

Terrence wanted to believe him, but neither of them knew the future. The dragon clan wouldn't be fine even if Irwin didn't go to the press. Irwin was still bent on attacking and killing all of them, and there was nothing anyone could do to stop him. The last thing Terrence wanted was to create trouble for the dragons, and while he suspected that Irwin would've found another reason to attack them if he and his family hadn't left, he didn't like the thought that Irwin would use them as an excuse.

But in this situation, he was powerless. The only thing he could do was wait and see what happened, no matter how much he hated it.

Donahue wished he could take all of this away from Terrence. It wasn't fair for Terrence to still have to deal with Irwin, and Donahue disliked everything he'd just heard.

He was proud of Terrence for standing up to Irwin, but he was worried. What if Irwin went to the press? Donahue had attempted to reassure Terrence that it wouldn't change anything even if he did, but he wasn't sure about that. Even if Elijah's journalist friend helped, there would still be people who thought Irwin was telling the truth and that the dragons needed to be investigated, or worse, kicked out of town.

It wouldn't be unheard of. After Donahue had moved in with the dragons, he'd poked around the Internet. Humans and shifters were supposed to have the same rights, but humans often found a way around that. Of course, Irwin wasn't human, so maybe no one would listen to him, especially after Curt had attacked the dragons.

There was proof of that. He hadn't been discreet, and journalists had camped out in front of the gate for days after the attack. They'd wanted to know what had happened, but Elijah's friend was the only one who'd gotten an exclusive interview. It had moved the public opinion and given the dragons the upper hand, but that might change at any moment, especially if Irwin was smart about it.

"I'm worried," Terrence admitted.

Donahue wanted to tell him everything would be all right, but could he? Even if he told him that, he doubted Terrence would believe him. After all, he was just a guy. He'd been living with the dragons for longer than Terrence, but he was human and technically an outsider. Donahue wanted to talk to Elijah about it, but he wasn't sure it was a good idea to do so now. Elijah already had more than enough to worry about. Would it be fair to burden him with Donahue's demands?

Donahue glanced at Terrence, who was still carefully cutting carrots. Even if he didn't want to talk to Elijah for himself, he wanted to do it for Terrence. He would have taken Terrence straight to Elijah's office if he hadn't known that Elijah was in a meeting.

Since they couldn't talk to him, Donahue would have to find another way to distract Terrence. That meant leaving the kitchen. He didn't want everyone staring at them while he did so.

He waved at Tim, who'd been sitting at a nearby table, talking to Lindsey. Tim narrowed his eyes when Donahue gestured at the vegetables and the cutting board Terrence was using.

"What do you want?" he asked, his tone careful.

"Can you take over? Terrence and I have something to do."

"We do?" Terrence asked.

Donahue hooked an arm around Terrence's. "Yes. We'll be outside if anyone needs us."

"What are we going to do outside?" Terrence asked as Donahue dragged him away from the counter and out of the kitchen.

"How long has it been since you shifted?"

Terrence's step faltered. "Since we were rescued."

"Even then, when you shifted, it was for an emergency, not to have fun."

"Yeah, but I can't shift."

Donahue paused next to the back door. "Why not?" *He* wouldn't be shifting, which meant he needed to stay warm. He grabbed one of the jackets hanging from the hooks, intent on putting it on, but he could see Terrence wasn't moving.

"Why wouldn't you shift? I might not be a shifter, but I've been around shifters long enough to know they feel better after they shift. It's been several days since you did, so I imagine your cockatrice wants out."

"It does, but it's better if I don't shift."

"Why?"

"Because the dragons have been fighting the cockatrices. What will they do if one of them suddenly appears on their front step?"

What he said made sense, but it wasn't fair, and Donahue didn't think Elijah intended to make it impossible for Terrence and his family to shift. He was a fair alpha, and he'd probably thought of this problem when he'd offered Terrence and his family a place here.

"I'm pretty sure that as long as we warn Elijah that you're shifting, there won't be a problem. He doesn't expect you and your family never to shift again."

"Maybe not never, but we should wait until the war is over."

"That could take weeks." If not months. But Donahue wasn't willing to consider that possibility. The war couldn't last months. Irwin was too impatient and wanted his reward.

Donahue took out his phone. There was only one way for Terrence to believe him, and even though he didn't want to bother the alpha, he didn't see a way out of it. He quickly dialed Elijah's number and put the call on speaker. Terrence tried to snatch the phone away from him, possibly to hang up, but before he could, Elijah answered.

"Yes?"

"Hey, sorry to bother you while you're in a meeting," Donahue said. "We just wanted to warn you that Terrence was going to shift, so if anyone sees a cockatrice flying around, they shouldn't be scared because we're not under attack."

Elijah didn't even hesitate. "Thank you for warning me. I'll send a group text so that everyone knows. Have fun."

That was it. Elijah didn't try to stop Terrence from shifting. He didn't even sound worried about it.

Donahue beamed at Terrence and hung up. "See? Now

let's go."

He grabbed a pair of boots he was pretty sure belonged to Olsen, pulled them on, and opened the door. He expected Terrence to be hesitant, but he followed him outside. He wore jeans and a sweater, and Donahue couldn't imagine taking them off to shift. The thought made him shiver, but he still watched as Terrence quickly stripped and dumped his clothes onto a bench. There were several of them placed there for this reason.

Donahue had been around long enough to have seen people shift back and forth many times. The dragons always seemed to have fun in their dragon form, even though they tried to stick to the area around the house. It couldn't be great for such big animals, but especially right now, they couldn't afford to go further. They might be attacked, and if they were, it would be nearly impossible to rescue them. The cockatrices had assaulted several dragon shifters recently. Some had been wounded so badly that they were still recovering. No one wanted that to happen again.

But none of that would be a problem today because they weren't going far. Donahue couldn't shift, and he had no intention of letting Terrence carry him around while he flew. He was fine with his feet on the ground, thank you very much. He hoped Terrence would eventually take him up again, but not now.

Terrence hesitated once he was naked. Donahue didn't say anything, knowing Terrence needed time. He was planning on pushing if Terrence changed his mind, but he didn't have to.

The shift was fast, just like for dragons. Terrence's body grew and changed. It was both mesmerizing and slightly horrifying. Terrence's arms became wings, his face elongated into a beak, and feathers sprouted on his head and down his spine. His feet grew claws that could kill a man, and when he raised his head to the sky, Donahue couldn't help but notice how long his neck was.

There was definitely some chicken in there.

Terrence opened his wings and shook them out. They were leathery, like a dragon's, with almost no feathers. Terrence didn't have many of them. There was a row from the middle of his forehead down his neck and the length of his spine, along with a bunch under his chin and on his chest. They were dark red, almost the color of blood. Donahue wondered if they were soft. There was only one way to find out.

He took one step closer. "Can I touch you?"

Tim was the only shifter he'd ever asked because he was Victor's boyfriend. He was family to Donahue, and he'd readily agreed. However, his dragon form differed from Terrence's cockatrice form, and Donahue was curious.

Terrence moved, closing his wings around his body. He lowered his head, stopping only when they were face to face, looking each other in the eyes. Donahue hoped it was a yes as he raised his hand and gently stroked his fingertips down the length of Terrence's beak.

It was hard and smooth like Donahue expected. Donahue could only imagine how easily it could kill someone, but he decided not to think about that. This moment was for them, not about the war, Irwin, or anything else.

He stroked up until his fingers touched feathers. They were soft, and Donahue laughed when Terrence shook his head and preened.

"Yes, you're a beautiful cockatrice," he confirmed.

And he wanted this beautiful cockatrice to be his desperately.

Terrence had wanted to shift, but he'd thought it would be better not to take the chance. The dragons had only just welcomed him and his family, and they weren't used to having to share their space with cockatrice shifters. Reminding them of what they could shift into sounded like the worst idea, but Terrence trusted Donahue. He might not be a dragon, but he'd lived here long enough to know how things worked and how people would react. Terrence was glad he'd pushed him to shift.

Donahue wouldn't have touched Terrence's cockatrice form if he hadn't. Terrence loved it.

He preened under Donahue's touch, wanting more in both his forms. He wanted to shift back and drag Donahue into his arms, but Donahue seemed fascinated by his cockatrice form. Terrence also wanted to fly but didn't know what option to choose.

He stepped closer, bumping his forehead against Donahue's chest. Donahue stumbled back and laughed, and when he gripped one of Terrence's wings, Terrence didn't complain.

"You're going to throw me to the ground if you're not careful," Donahue said. "Now, as much as I want to continue petting you, I'm kind of cold, so I'll go back inside."

Terrence didn't like that. He looked from Donahue to the sky until Donahue understood what he was asking.

He shook his head. "Not this time. We can fly together when it's not as cold and after discussing how it works. I don't want to repeat the experience of the last time we flew together."

Because Terrence had needed to snatch him up with his claws and fly with him dangling under him.

It had to have been terrifying. Cockatrice shifters only had their back legs and feet to grab stuff when they were in that form. Unlike dragons, who had separate wings, cockatrices' wings were also their arms. That meant Terrence had nothing to use to grab Donahue if they flew together. Donahue could climb on his back, but he was right that they needed to talk about it first.

Terrence wanted to fly but didn't want to leave Donahue alone. Thankfully, Donahue seemed to understand, and he gently pushed Terrence away. "Fly. I'll sit on this bench, freezing my ass off and waiting for you. Just don't take too long, all right?"

Terrence tried to lead Donahue toward the door. He should go inside if he wasn't going to fly with him.

But Donahue was stubborn and pushed back. "I'll go inside if I can't take it anymore, but I don't want you to worry about me. Focus on yourself." He leaned forward and smacked a kiss on Terrence's beak. "Have fun."

Terrence was done arguing. He quickly moved back, glanced one last time at Donahue, and opened his wings. He pushed with his back legs, getting himself in the air.

It was like coming home. It *was* coming home. Just like dragons, cockatrice shifters belonged in the air. Terrence didn't need to shift, but when he didn't shift, he missed it. He belonged both on the ground and in the air, and he couldn't ignore that.

Even though he wanted nothing more than to fly, he reminded himself that Donahue was waiting for him. He gave himself a quick workout, enjoying the feeling of the cold air sliding over his body. He kept an eye open in case Irwin attacked, but no one was around, not even dragon shifters. They'd probably decided to keep their distance after they'd found out that Terrence was shifting.

Terrence didn't want them to stay away, but it was probably a good idea for his first time shifting here. It gave him space to do what he wanted without having to fear scaring someone.

This was new for him. He'd never had to worry about what the people around him would think about him shifting, and now, he did. He didn't mind, though. He liked his new life's opportunities and didn't want to ruin it. He wanted to feel at home here, settle down, and, if he was lucky, start a relationship with Donahue.

He was pretty sure Donahue would be on board, but he didn't want to start anything until he felt a bit more secure. To do so, he needed to talk to Elijah.

The alpha had been clear that he considered Terrence and his family clan members, but Terrence wanted to contribute. It would be expected of him if he was a clan member, and he didn't like that Elijah was using kids' gloves with him. He'd been tense and afraid for a long time, but he wasn't anymore. He was ready to start living the way he should always have.

He hadn't had nearly enough flying time when he lowered toward the ground. He could see Donahue on the bench where he'd left his clothes, a blanket wrapped around his shoulders. He looked good waiting for Terrence, and Terrence could imagine himself coming back to this every day for the rest of his life.

Some might think it was too fast, but Donahue had been there when Terrence believed everything was lost. He'd comforted him, even though Terrence had been an enemy. He'd even protected him when the guards had wanted to hurt him.

Donahue was a wonderful man, and Terrence wanted to be able to call him his. Now that he wasn't with Irwin anymore, he didn't have to avoid relationships and love. He could throw himself into it and start building a future with someone.

With Donahue.

He landed in front of the house. Donahue rushed toward him instantly, holding out a blanket. He wrapped it around Terrence's shoulders when Terrence shifted back and rubbed up and down Terrence's arms to warm him up. Terrence could have told him that he wasn't cold yet, but he was enjoying the moment too much, so he kept his mouth shut and basked in the attention.

"You need to get dressed," Donahue said as he guided Terrence toward the bench.

Terrence wanted to kiss Donahue but didn't want to freeze his ass off, so he obeyed. He quickly got dressed, and once his clothes were on, he wrapped the blanket around his shoulders again. He wasn't ready to go back inside, which meant he needed to stay warm. Donahue still had a blanket wrapped around his jacket, so he should be fine for a moment longer.

"Let's go in and get you something warm to drink," Donahue said as he turned.

Terrence grabbed his wrist and pulled him back. Donahue stumbled and fell forward, but it was okay because Terrence was there to catch him. He wrapped his arms around Donahue, then gave Donahue time to step away if he didn't want this.

He should have known better. Donahue grinned at him, clearly happy about the situation.

"Finally," he murmured.

It hit Terrence then that Donahue had been waiting for him. That was why he hadn't kissed him again. He'd made his interest clear, but he'd wanted Terrence to take the next step.

He did.

He lowered his face as he pulled Donahue harder against him. He hooked one arm around Donahue's waist, the other going up so he could cup a hand around the back of Donahue's head. There was no resistance as Terrence pulled them together. Their lips met, and Terrence sighed in pleasure at the sensation of coming home.

This was his home now, and not only the house and the clan. Donahue would be Terrence's home, too, if Terrence played his cards right.

He'd never liked card games, but this wasn't a game. It was life, and Terrence wanted Donahue. He was pretty sure Donahue wanted him just as much, which was a relief because he wasn't willing to let go. Donahue felt like he belonged in Terrence's arms.

His lips were soft, his tongue slick, and his body hard. Terrence wanted to take so much more, but a kiss was enough for now. He needed to talk to Elijah and allow himself to relax and settle before he could offer Donahue what he deserved.

But he was done waiting to see what would happen. It was time for him to start living his life, and he could only do that if he took the next step forward.

CHAPTER ELEVEN

Donahue hadn't been surprised when Terrence had told him he wanted to talk to Elijah. He wanted the same, so they'd decided to ask for a meeting during which they could both explain what they wanted and needed and pray that Elijah would give it to them.

Because Donahue wasn't going anywhere. If this was Terrence's home, Donahue was staying. He hadn't wanted to leave before but wanted to even less now that he and Terrence were together.

They hadn't discussed it, but Donahue knew what he wanted, and he suspected Terrence felt the same. Maybe he wanted to wait until they both knew what the future held and were secure in their place with the clan, but that was all right. It would be better for both of them to know where they stood before they got too serious. Donahue didn't think he could stand having his heart broken just because he had to leave and Terrence wanted to stay.

"You don't have to be so tense," he told Terrence as he raised their hands.

His fingers were intertwined with Terrence's, so Donahue took advantage of it and kissed the back of Terrence's hand. Terrence's fingers tightened, but when he tried to smile, it was clear he hadn't relaxed one bit.

Donahue hadn't expected him to. Of course he was tense. Donahue was, too. It was scary to have this meeting, but they both needed it. Besides, Donahue doubted it would go badly. Elijah had welcomed them into the clan without conditions except that Terrence had to give him as much information about Irwin and the cockatrices as he could, which Terrence would have done anyway.

"What if he decides he made a mistake and wants me to leave?" Terrence asked.

"I don't see why he would. Elijah might make mistakes, but when he does, he admits it and fixes them."

"Fixing them might mean kicking me out."

"He won't kick you out," Donahue insisted. "That's not the kind of person he is. He knew what he was doing when he welcomed you into the clan, and he won't change his mind. Besides, you've been here long enough now that people are used to your presence. There might be some who aren't happy, but they're a minority, and Elijah is the alpha. They can either go along with his orders or leave."

"That doesn't feel fair, even though I know it's how it works."

"In this case, they're wrong if they don't want you here, so I don't care if they decide to go."

He really didn't. He had no patience for people who didn't want Terrence and his family there just because of what they could shift into. He'd understand if they didn't like them as people, but they didn't even know them because they refused to get anywhere near them. It was ridiculous and childish, and Donahue had already snapped at a few people he'd caught gossiping behind Terrence's back.

But he couldn't think about that now. He and Terrence had reached Elijah's office door, and it was time for their meeting.

Except there was already someone inside. The door wasn't closed all the way, but even if it had been, Donahue and Terrence would have heard the conversation because whoever was there was yelling.

"I just can't believe they want me to do that," a man complained.

Donahue frowned. "I'm pretty sure that's Gunther."

"Gunther?"

"He's a mage and Elijah's friend. He's been helping Valerian since he's both a mage and a psychic and spending quite a bit of time here."

Donahue couldn't hear Elijah's answer, but Gunther's voice was clear and loud.

"It doesn't make sense unless they don't want to be allied with you, and why wouldn't they?" Gunther asked. "They're even threatening to kick me out if I don't take a step back. Don't they understand how serious this is and that Valerian needs help and training? Why would they want him not to get it?"

Donahue's stomach churned. Whatever the problem was, it didn't sound good.

Gunther wasn't a clan member. He had a coven, and Donahue suspected that Elijah had hoped they would step in when it was time to fight the cockatrices. Irwin had a coven on his side, and Elijah must've hoped he would have one, too. He'd been wrong from the sound of it, which could be a problem. The dragons needed all the help they could get, and right now, that help was a bunch of psychics and two PIs.

It didn't feel like enough.

"I know," Gunther said, his voice softer now. "I'm sorry, and I'll try talking to them. They can't just do this and expect me to go along with it."

There was a murmur when Elijah spoke. Gunther was quick to answer.

"I'll let you know what happens and keep you up to date. I'm sorry I took so much of your time when you have meetings."

The sound of footsteps coming toward the door made Donahue jump. He and Terrence exchanged a guilty look as the door opened.

Gunther blinked at them. He looked from Donahue to Terrence, then sighed and nodded. "Sorry about that. I had some things to say."

"We heard," Donahue said. "I'm sorry your coven is being a bunch of dickheads."

Gunther laughed. "That's one way to put it. Don't worry about me, though. I'll be fine."

Donahue hoped he would be. They weren't friends but were friendly, and he liked the mage. It wasn't just that the dragons needed Gunther. It didn't feel fair to ask him to step back when he was Elijah's friend.

"Come in," Elijah called out.

Gunther stepped into the hallway. Donahue tugged Terrence into the office, needing this to be over and to ask questions he hoped Elijah would answer.

"Why don't you sit down?" Elijah asked, waving at the chairs on the other side of his desk. "Tell me what's going on."

Donahue and Terrence looked at each other. One of them needed to start. It might as well be Donahue.

He turned his focus back to Elijah. "I was talking to Olsen recently, and he said he talked to you about becoming a clan member and staying here permanently. I know you didn't offer that when you welcomed us into your home, but I'd like the same opportunity."

"You want to become a clan member?" Elijah asked.

"I would love to. I enjoy living here and the sense of family I get from the clan. I know I might not bring a lot, but I'll help in any way I can, and as soon as this mess is over, I'll start working. I might be a burden right now, but I won't be forever."

Donahue was really selling himself, wasn't he? He felt ridiculous, but it was better if Elijah knew his feelings and thoughts.

"You're not a burden, and I'd be delighted to welcome you

into the clan," Elijah said with a smile. "If you want to stay permanently, you're welcome to do so. We'd be happy to have you. We already are."

Donahue smiled back. This was what he'd wanted. He'd be allowed to stay even after the war with the cockatrices ended. He could breathe, relax, and tell himself that he wouldn't be going anywhere as long as they survived.

He hadn't needed another incentive to make sure the dragons won the war, but he had one now, and he'd do everything he could to have the future he yearned for.

"Thank you so much," he told Elijah.

"I should have been clearer when you and your family first arrived. I realize that we had you move here because it would be safer for you considering the situation, but I already see you as part of the clan. I should have told you, and of course, if Roslin and your parents wish to stay, they're welcome to."

"I'll tell them." Donahue suspected that his parents would want to keep the clan house as a home base and start traveling more, but he didn't know what Roslin would decide. It was good to know he had options and that whatever happened, this would always be a home for him and the rest of the family.

Elijah turned to Terrence. "What about you? Are you here to support Donahue, or was there anything you wanted to talk about?"

Terrence bounced his knee a few times. "I wanted to talk about my place in the clan. I know I'm already a clan member, but I'd like to contribute. I feel that some of the people who are unhappy about my presence here feel that way because I'm not doing anything."

"You don't have to do anything to be a clan member."

"Maybe not, but it would be easier for them to accept me if I were productive. I realize I can't be allowed to leave clan territory as long as Irwin is a problem, but there has to be something I can do."

"As far as I'm concerned, you're already doing enough by telling me what you think Irwin is up to."

That was news to Donahue. "What *do* you think he is up to?" he asked.

"Right now, he's seething. He wants to attack, but he's not impulsive like Curt was, and he knows that even if he won, it would be with heavy losses. He has a weapon now, though. He'll need time to coordinate with the coven, but eventually, they'll find a way to work together."

And that was when the problems would start.

Terrence wished he was wrong, but he knew Irwin. He'd worked with him for years, and he'd known him since he was born. The man wasn't impulsive, and he wasn't an idiot. He knew what he wanted, and if it meant getting it, he would wait and plan.

Terrence was sure that was what Irwin was doing. Even though he wanted to drag Terrence and his family back and make sure they paid for running away, he'd bide his time. He'd make sure he'd have his revenge eventually, which was why he wasn't in a hurry.

Terrence would make sure Irwin never put his hands on anyone in his family ever again. Hell, he'd make sure Irwin could never hurt a dragon again. He didn't care what Irwin believed about the dragons. They'd welcomed Terrence and his family, and as far as he was concerned, it made them the good guys. It would have been easy for Elijah to torture the information he wanted out of Terrence and kill him, leaving his family in Irwin's hands. Instead, he'd listened to him and offered him a choice.

Terrence would never be able to thank Elijah enough for what he'd done, but he'd try. His first goal was to make sure the dragons won the war.

"How long will it take him to trust the coven enough to work with them?" Elijah asked.

"That's anyone's guess. I don't think he'll ever fully trust the mages, to be honest. He doesn't trust anyone but himself, not even his son. He's angry, though, so I wouldn't be surprised if he forced himself to go through with whatever they're planning just because he wants revenge. He thinks he's stronger than the dragons, anyway. I'm sure he believes that he can do this if he has the coven's help."

Elijah leaned back in his chair. It was clear he didn't like what Terrence had told him, but unlike Irwin would have, he wasn't yelling and threatening people. He was thinking about the problem.

"What we need is information," Donahue said. "We could use Kenneth."

Elijah nodded. "We already are. He's been hanging around Irwin, listening to his conversations. So far, he doesn't have anything concrete. Thankfully, Curt's girlfriend doesn't seem to be around. Do you know what happened to her?" Elijah asked, turning to Terrence.

Terrence shook his head. "I wouldn't be surprised if Irwin's hurt her. She was Curt's girlfriend, and Curt betrayed Irwin."

"She might not have had anything to do with that."

"Irwin wouldn't have wanted to risk it even if she didn't. As strong as he believes he is, he's always terrified someone will attempt to take his place as the alpha. He probably thought that was what Curt was aiming for, and I don't know if he was, but in the end, it doesn't matter. Irwin killed Curt because he was putting the clan in danger and acting as if the clan was his. I have no doubt that Curt's girlfriend is either imprisoned or dead." And he didn't really care.

She wasn't a good person. She'd worked with Curt, and

Terrence had been close enough to Valerian to see what those two did to him. She might not have been the one physically hurting Valerian, but she'd supported Curt, and for Terrence, that was enough to know that the world was a better place without her. The fact that it took away one of their enemies was a bonus.

"We'll know as soon as Irwin decides what to do next," Elijah reassured Terrence and Donahue. "In the meantime, we're working on strengthening our bonds with other communities in the city. They know that if Irwin manages to get rid of us, he'll turn to them next, and they don't want that."

"Not everyone seems happy to help you," Terrence pointed out.

"You heard what Gunther said."

It wasn't a question, but Terrence nodded. "It would be good to have a coven on our side. I don't know much about the mages helping Irwin, but they have a reputation."

"They do, and I promise I'm working on finding as many allies as possible. It takes time, so Irwin's delay is good for us."

It was, but Irwin wouldn't wait for much longer. Terrence had dealt him a personal affront, and he wanted revenge. Terrence knew that if Irwin ever got his hands on him, he'd die a painful and slow death.

He still didn't regret taking his family away. He never would, even if he died.

"I don't want either of you to worry too much," Elijah said as he leaned forward. "The situation isn't ideal, but I'm doing everything I can. I don't know if it'll be enough, but I'll fight as hard as I have to in order to save the clan. I was the one who created this home. I won't let anything happen, no matter what I have to do."

Terrence believed him. Elijah was such a different alpha compared to Irwin. For Irwin, only what he wanted mattered.

He viewed his clan as people who were supposed to serve him, and he was proud of it. He was proud of the power he wielded over them and how he could make them do things just because he said so. Elijah, on the other hand, cared about the clan. He wanted to keep them safe, even if it meant his death. He was ready to reach out to people who wanted nothing to do with him. He wouldn't care as long as it meant they had allies.

Terrence didn't know if they would win, but they deserved to. Irwin, on the other hand, only deserved to die.

There was nothing more to say, so Terrence and Donahue left Elijah to his next meeting. The alpha looked tired but determined. He wouldn't stop until he was sure his clan was safe.

Terrence still didn't have a job, and he suspected that Elijah had avoided giving him one on purpose. He probably wanted to have Terrence on hand in case anything happened, but it still left Terrence uneasy. Maybe he could help more in the kitchen or in the yard. Everyone took turns cleaning the communal areas and cooking, but Terrence felt he had something to prove. He wanted the dragons to see that he took this seriously and truly was a clan member.

He'd find a way to do so. He was determined to make this place his home.

Hopefully, with Donahue by his side.

Donahue had been sure everything would be all right. He hadn't told Terrence that because he'd known Terrence wouldn't believe it until Elijah told him himself.

He had. Terrence had been doubtful about his place with the dragon clan and had asked Elijah about it. Elijah had reassured him that he and his family were clan members. It didn't matter that they were cockatrice shifters or that some of the dragons weren't happy. Elijah had made his decision, and he wouldn't go back on it.

Terrence was visibly more relaxed, and Donahue had a hard time not staring. As they walked side by side down the hallways, headed toward his bedroom, he almost couldn't believe it was the same man who'd been so hesitant and worried just half an hour ago.

"You can say it, you know," Terrence said.

Donahue blinked at him. "Say what?"

"That you knew everything would be all right and that I was worrying for nothing. I could tell you wanted to tell me earlier, but you didn't."

Donahue knocked their shoulders together. "Because I could tell it wouldn't help."

"Maybe not, but you did know everything would be all right."

"Only because I know Elijah better than you do. I've been here for a while, and I've seen him making the kind of decision that changed people's lives. I knew that if he'd offered you and your family to stay here and become clan members, he wouldn't go back on that decision. He believes it's the right thing to do, and that's that."

"Do you believe the same, too?"

Donahue didn't want to come on too strongly. After all, they didn't know each other well, and Terrence probably still felt like he wasn't quite stable. It would take him some time to get used to being a member of a dragon clan, going from living only with his family to sharing a house with a bunch of dragon shifters and psychics, and even more so, to wrap his mind around the fact that he and his family were finally safe after so many years fighting Irwin.

But Donahue also didn't want to hide how he felt about Terrence. He'd been fascinated by him since Terrence had appeared at the gate, wanting to tell Elijah what Irwin was plotting. Most people wouldn't have warned the dragons. It had been dangerous, and Terrence hadn't only risked his own life but also the life of his sister, brother, and father. He'd done it anyway because it had been the right thing. Donahue had been impressed, and he still was. Terrence was the kind of guy he wanted in his life.

And he had him.

He didn't have any problems taking things slowly, but he also wouldn't mind going a bit faster. It would all depend on Terrence and how he took what Donahue had organized for tonight.

Finding privacy in a house where so many people lived wasn't always easy. Donahue would never move out unless he was forced to, but that didn't mean he loved all aspects of living here. Luckily, his bedroom was more like a suite than a single room. It had a nice balcony and a small sitting area. He didn't need anything more. He'd never been a great cook, so he was glad he could just go downstairs and grab food when he was hungry. His place might become a bit cramped if someone else ever moved in, but it wasn't something Donahue needed to worry about yet. Now that Terrence was a clan member, they had all the time they needed to get to know each other better and, hopefully, to let their relationship grow.

Donahue grinned. "I *know* it was the right decision to make."

Clearly that was what Terrence needed to hear — he relaxed and smiled at Donahue. He didn't often smile, maybe because of how hard his life had been until now, but Donahue didn't mind. It just meant he'd have to put a smile on Terrence's face as often as he could.

He was ready to take on the challenge. "Do you have to go back to your bedroom?" he asked.

"Not really. Joe is still nervous and wants to have us all in his line of sight all the time, but he needs to accept that we're

138

clan members and that no one here will hurt any of us. It'll do him good to see that I can stay out of our rooms without anything happening to me."

If Donahue had things his way, many things would be happening to Terrence, but he didn't say that out loud. "So you wouldn't mind spending some time with me?" Donahue wouldn't ask Terrence to spend the night. He wanted him to, but Terrence would want to check on his family before going to bed. Donahue didn't want him to have to make a choice, so it would be better to just see what happened if Terrence said he wanted to spend at least the evening with him.

"What do you have in mind?" Terrence asked.

Luckily, they were almost at Donahue's room. He'd set up everything earlier with the intent of seducing Terrence and spending some time with him, and that hadn't changed. It would be easier for Terrence to relax now that he knew he wasn't going anywhere.

Donahue opened his bedroom door and waved Terrence inside. "Let me show you."

Terrence looked around the room. Donahue had been here for a while, and he'd made himself at home. It wasn't dirty, but it was messy, with clothes draped over a chair by the bed and a few knickknacks around. Donahue had made the bed, though. He wanted to make a good impression, even if Terrence didn't spend the night.

As much as he wanted to drag Terrence to the bed, he gestured at the glass door instead. "I know it's February and that it's cold, but I have plenty of blankets. I thought we could eat a snack on the balcony and look at the stars."

Terrence blinked at him, and Donahue wondered what he was thinking. Was this too much? Probably. Donahue was often too much, so he wouldn't be surprised if Terrence said no.

But Terrence smiled, and all of Donahue's doubts flew out the window.

"I'd like that. I'll take those blankets you mentioned, though. I don't particularly like being cold."

Donahue didn't think anyone enjoyed being cold, but he'd make sure Terrence wasn't.

He opened the balcony door, grabbed all the blankets he'd put in a basket next to the door, and wrapped one around Terrence's shoulders. He gestured at Terrence to sit down and went to work once he was in the chair.

By the time Donahue was done with him, Terrence was just a head poking from a mountain of blankets. Donahue might have gone overboard because he hadn't kept even one blanket for himself.

Terrence looked down at himself and grinned. "I see you have snacks, but I don't think I'll be able to eat them if I can't use my hands."

Donahue dropped into the other chair and smiled back. "I'll feed you."

Terrence's eyes widened a bit. Donahue reminded himself that Terrence wasn't used to this kind of thing. He'd avoided relationships because it had been better while he still lived with the cockatrices, and he probably didn't know how to take Donahue's exuberance. Donahue didn't know how to deal with the bubbly way Terrence made him feel, either.

The snack he'd put together wasn't much. He hadn't been sure how long Terrence would want to stick around, so he'd put together a charcuterie board that was heavy on cheese because he loved cheese.

Who didn't?

Initially, the conversation was slow going, mostly because they were both eating, but that was fine. Donahue didn't need every moment to be filled with words. As long as Terrence was here with him, he was fine feeding him and staring at the stars, even though he felt kind of cold since all his blankets were on Terrence.

"What do I call you?" he asked.

"I'm sure you remember that my name is Terrence," Terrence teased.

"Maybe I could call you Terry."

Terrence grimaced. "Don't even try."

His grumpy expression made Donahue laugh. "All right. I just wanted to know how to introduce you. Are you my partner? That feels a bit serious for what we have. Boyfriend's juvenile, but it does fit better."

Terrence extracted a hand from under the mountain of blankets. It took him a moment, but he took one of Donahue's hands once it was free. "You're freezing," he murmured.

"It's fine," Donahue reassured him.

"It's not fine. I'm not going to let my boyfriend freeze his ass off when there's a perfectly good bedroom on the other side of this door. Let's go inside. We'll both be more comfortable."

Donahue wasn't going to argue any more than he already had because he was *fucking freezing*. He grabbed everything he didn't want to leave outside overnight and got it inside. His face hurt, and his skin felt like it was thawing. It prickled in an unpleasant way.

He rubbed his face as he turned and watched Terrence unwrap himself from the bundle of blankets. He was still wearing his jeans and sweater, but Donahue was up for more.

"Do you know the best way to warm up someone?" he asked.

"Something tells me you're teasing, but please. Tell me."

"Skin to skin. Haven't you ever read a romance novel?"

Terrence laughed. "Not really. I never had a lot of time to read, but if this is what happens in those books, maybe I should. It could give me good ideas to use with you."

Donahue loved that Terrence was teasing him back. He also loved that Terrence didn't seem cowed by his idea, not even when he took off his sweater. Terrence quickly followed his lead, and while Donahue wanted to stare at his brand-new boyfriend, he actually *was* cold.

As soon as he was naked, he dove into his bed and wrapped the blankets around his body. The problem was that there was no heat under them. Donahue's body was too cold, and it would take time for it to warm up the bed.

But Terrence didn't have that problem. When he slid under the blankets, Donahue could feel his heat. He moved toward him, eager to share.

When Donahue plastered his body against Terrence's, Terrence hissed and scrambled backward. Donahue would have none of that. He wrapped his arms and legs around his boyfriend's body, needing to feel warm. Luckily for him, he'd never been shy, so he had no trouble with Terrence feeling his naked skin.

"It's like hugging a giant ice statue," Terrence complained.

Donahue didn't miss the way Terrence was rubbing his hands up and down over his skin to warm him. It made him feel all fluttery inside. "Well, the sooner you warm me up, the sooner I'll stop feeling that way."

"What did you have in mind?" Terrence asked, his voice almost a purr.

Did cockatrice shifters purr? It felt like they shouldn't since they were a mix of reptile and bird, but Donahue was eager to find out. He was ready to sacrifice himself for that experiment.

He leaned closer to kiss Terrence. Terrence opened his mouth to him instantly, welcoming him in. His mouth was warm and slick and made Donahue want to lose himself in his heat.

Or maybe that was because he was still really fucking cold.

But it didn't last long. One of Terrence's hands snuck between them, abandoning Donahue's back and moving around him. Donahue was thrilled when it landed on his dick. That would definitely warm him up.

He groaned in pleasure when Terrence wrapped his hands around both their cocks. Their bodies were tangled together, and the closeness made him feel like they were one. It was cheesy, but Donahue was thrilled.

He wanted to feel as if they were one. He wanted Terrence in his life, and he was all in, even though they didn't know each other well. Maybe it was instinct, or maybe Donahue was a fool who read too many romance novels. He didn't feel it mattered. He just knew that Terrence was it for him, and he had no intention of ever letting him go unless that was what Terrence wanted.

And Donahue really hoped he would never want that.

"You feel so good," Terrence murmured.

He tightened his hand around them as he moved it up and down. Donahue didn't feel cold anymore. He felt like he was on fire as he clung to his boyfriend and kissed him. It was perfection, and the knowledge that he'd have this for the rest of his life made him grin like an idiot. Luckily, it seemed that Terrence already knew him well enough to realize this was normal. Donahue was happy and wasn't afraid to show it, especially to Terrence.

They moved together, pushing each other closer to release as their bodies learned what the other enjoyed. Donahue was sure he would have liked anything Terrence wanted to do with him, but this was perfect for their first time together. It wasn't rushed, and there was no expectation except the one that they'd both come by the time this was over.

Donahue was pretty sure they would.

He hadn't wanted to push Terrence and didn't feel like he was. Terrence was clearly enjoying himself as much as Donahue if his blissful expression and the choppy way he moved were any indication. Donahue wanted to push him even further, but he wasn't quite sure how to do that. He didn't know Terrence well enough yet.

He told Terrence how much he loved this, that he wanted to do it again soon, and that they would since Terrence was home now. Terrence shuddered at every word that came out of Donahue's mouth, and when he buried his face against Donahue's neck, Donahue knew he'd nailed it.

But Terrence didn't come yet. Instead, he squeezed their cocks and moved his hand faster. Knowing that he was capable of pleasuring his boyfriend with his words thrilled Donahue in a way few other things did. Between that, Terrence's hand on his cock, and Terrence's lips on his skin, Donahue didn't have a chance.

When his orgasm slammed into him, he grabbed Terrence's head and kissed him hard. Their teeth clanked together painfully, but Donahue ignored it because this was what he'd wanted when he'd thought of this evening. Terrence was in his arms, and he was his. Donahue was never letting go.

Except he had to when Terrence laughed and tickled him.

"I draw the line at tickling," Donahue warned him.

"Then you should have let me go sooner."

Donahue pouted. "How can I? I don't want you to leave the bed."

Terrence pressed a kiss against Donahue's sweaty chest. "I'm not going far. I just don't want us to be stuck together tomorrow morning."

"Does that mean you're spending the night?"

"Unless you're going to kick me out."

"Not even if you ask me to. You're stuck with me."

From the soft smile Terrence gave him, Donahue was pretty sure he didn't mind.

CHAPTER TWELVE

Donahue couldn't stop smiling, and people were starting to notice. His brother was sitting next to him on the couch, scrolling on his phone, but he kept glancing at Donahue. He clearly had something to say, but Donahue wouldn't make things easy on him. If Olsen had questions, he could ask. In the meantime, Donahue would be here, grinning like an idiot as he trawled the Internet.

He was checking the main news websites to see how the humans were talking about the cockatrices and dragons. For now, it seemed they'd forgotten there had been an attack on the dragon clan. They'd gone back to talking about other things, and it was both a relief and annoying.

Didn't they understand how traumatizing this had been for the dragons? They'd been attacked in their own home. Dragons had died defending their home and the people who lived there. How could no one remember that?

"You're creeping me out," Olsen eventually declared.

Donahue smiled even wider and put down his phone as he turned toward his brother. "Why?"

Olsen waved his hand at Donahue's face. "That smile. You look almost manic."

"I feel like I should be offended. Why don't you want me to be happy?"

"I do want you to be happy. It would just be great if you could do it less creepily."

But Donahue *couldn't* stop smiling. Even knowing a war was brewing, he didn't think he'd ever been as happy as he

145

was now. "Fine. I'll stop smiling since my baby brother can't take it."

Olsen punched Donahue's shoulder. "Just tell me what you're up to that makes you smile like that. I want the same."

"Then you need to find a hot boyfriend."

"Oh? Is that how it is?"

Donahue was about to answer when Kenneth barged into the living room through the wall, making him jump. His first reaction was to glare at the ghost, but it didn't last long when he saw Kenneth's expression. He got to his feet. "What is it?"

Olsen grumbled but got up, too. "Who is it? Kenneth?" he asked.

Donahue nodded but kept his focus on Kenneth. The ghost's expression made it clear that something was going on.

"The cockatrices are on the move," Kenneth announced.

Donahue swore and picked up his phone. He texted Terrence to let him know what was happening as he rushed out the door toward Elijah's office. That would be faster than calling. Elijah would send a group text so everyone in the clan knew something was happening.

Olsen and Kenneth followed Donahue. Even though Olsen couldn't see the ghost, he could tell something had happened.

"Kenneth said the cockatrices are on the move," Donahue told him. "Let the rest of the family know."

Olsen's expression was grim as he nodded. He took his phone out and got to work as they moved through the house. Luckily, Elijah's office wasn't far. The door was closed, and Donahue hoped he wouldn't be interrupting anything as he quickly knocked, then opened the door without waiting for an answer.

He blinked when he saw Elijah and Gunther sitting on one of the couches under the window. They were closer than he'd ever seen them, and Elijah had a hand on Gunther's thigh. They didn't look guilty or like they were trying to hide a relationship. Gunther looked as though he might be about to cry, so it was clear that Elijah had been comforting him. Donahue was still curious about what was going on between them, but now wasn't the moment to ask.

To be fair, he didn't think there would be a good moment to ask. It was none of his business, no matter how curious he was.

"Sorry for coming in like this, but Kenneth is with me. He told me that the cockatrices are on the move."

Both Gunther and Elijah shot to their feet. "Are they coming here?" Elijah asked as he grabbed his phone from the desk.

Donahue turned to Kenneth. The ghost nodded with a grim expression. "He wants to confront Elijah and keeps talking about Terrence."

Donahue didn't like that. He wanted to protect Terrence but couldn't keep his boyfriend away from this mess. As soon as Terrence heard what was happening, he would want to be there and confront Irwin.

The problem was that the cockatrice alpha knew how to get under Terrence's skin. He'd done it with the many phone calls and when Terrence had finally answered, so Donahue wouldn't be surprised if he did it today, too.

"I warned everyone," Elijah declared. "How long until they're here?"

Donahue looked at Kenneth, who shrugged. "I stayed for as long as I could because I wanted information, but they were leaving when I came back," Kenneth explained.

"Probably not long," Donahue told Elijah. "They're on their way already."

"I'm going down to the gate."

Donahue wasn't surprised. Elijah's main goal was to protect his people and his home, and he wouldn't hesitate to face Irwin to do that.

"I'm coming with you," he said.

He was glad when Elijah didn't forbid him to come. He wouldn't be of use in a physical fight, but Kenneth would be with Elijah, so the alpha needed someone to talk to the ghost. Donahue wasn't the only one who could do so, but he was right here and knew what was happening.

His mother was going to kill him when she found out about this.

They rushed through the house with Gunther behind them. He didn't look sad anymore, but rather, determined. Donahue had noticed him making a brief phone call and wondered who he'd called. His coven? Donahue knew they weren't happy with how much time Gunther was spending here and with the fact that he was open about supporting the dragons, but right now, he didn't seem to care.

Elijah was on his phone, too. Donahue didn't know who he was calling, but he could take a guess as he listened.

"You can't get here quickly enough, and even if you could, it's too dangerous," Elijah said. "I'll put the phone on speaker. You can record the call if you want proof of what's happening." He lowered his phone and tapped the screen.

A male voice came from it seconds later. "You shouldn't confront them. They're dangerous. I saw how many things they've done when I dug into them and their alpha for my article. He's not a good guy, Elijah."

"I'm aware of that. I have to protect my people and won't hide in my office while they fight for me."

This had to be the journalist Elijah had contacted after Curt's attack. Donahue couldn't remember his name, but he didn't care right now. If he'd guessed right, Elijah wanted this guy to listen and report on what was happening. It was the only way to make sure the truth was out there, but even then, Donahue wasn't sure it would matter. Humans only paid attention to what interested them and only believed what they wanted. Even when the truth was right in front of them, they often couldn't accept it. It was almost impossible to change someone's mind, especially when they weren't willing to listen and accept they could be wrong.

When they got outside, Donahue could see a small crowd had already gathered at the gate. He was glad to see that his family was nowhere to be seen, but he didn't like that Terrence was there, even though he wasn't surprised. He wished he could shield his boyfriend from what was about to happen, but he wouldn't. For one, it was too late, but even if it hadn't been, Terrence deserved to know what was happening. Even now that he wasn't part of the cockatrice clan anymore, he'd lived there all his life.

Donahue made a beeline for him. Terrence jumped when he pressed a hand against his back, then relaxed when he saw who it was. Together, they watched Elijah make his way toward the gate.

Once Elijah stood there, he turned to face the gathered people. "I want most of the people here to go back inside. Only the guards are to stay out."

People started grumbling. Donahue understood. They wanted to stay behind and protect their home, and Elijah was telling them not to. Donahue wasn't going anywhere since Kenneth was still hanging around, and he could tell by Terrence's expression that he wasn't moving, either. Everyone else did step back, though, which was a relief. Elijah had enough to worry about without adding his people to the bunch.

"They're here," Kenneth said.

Terrence was terrified, and he didn't mind admitting it. He was sure Donahue would understand if he told him, but he didn't have the occasion to do so because Kenneth was right.

Irwin was here.

Terrence hadn't known what to expect when Donahue texted him that Irwin was on his way. It seemed like a weird move on his part. Was he here to attack? Or was he plotting something else? There had to be a good reason for this, but Terrence couldn't begin to guess what it was.

The cockatrices landed in front of the gate. Terrence would have recognized Irwin's cockatrice form anywhere. Irwin was the first to reach them. More cockatrices landed behind him, but Irwin was the only one who shifted back to his human form.

Terrence understood why Irwin had flown rather than used a car, but he couldn't help but wonder if it was worth standing there in front of the dragons completely naked in the cold. It would have been awkward to bring his clothes and get dressed, but it didn't look like they were here to attack, since he was shifting.

Terrence didn't understand. If they weren't here to attack, *why* were they here?

Things got worse when he noticed people sliding off the backs of some of the cockatrices. Since they were in human form, it had to mean they couldn't shift, which in turn had to mean they were part of the coven. Terrence kept an eye on them but wasn't sure he could continue doing so when Irwin finally started talking.

"I didn't expect a welcome committee," he drawled.

All signs of surprise were gone from his expression. It was hard as he looked around, silently defying anyone to say something.

"Why are you here?" Elijah asked, his tone mirroring Irwin's expression.

"Hello to you too, Elijah."

"I don't have any patience for you, Irwin. What do you want?"

"I can tell you what he wants," Valerian said as he pushed forward in the crowd.

Terrence almost grabbed him to drag him back. What did he think he was doing?

Cooper seemed to feel the same as Terrence because his expression was grim, and he stood so close to Valerian that he might as well have been hugging him. Valerian didn't pause, though. He moved until he was next to Elijah, and both of them faced Irwin and the cockatrices. He seemed strong and confident, which was impressive because Terrence was shaking in his shoes.

"I know some of these people," Valerian said. "They hunted me and my family long enough that I'd recognize them anywhere."

Terrence was right. The coven was here, possibly to get Valerian back. If that was the reason for their presence, it meant a fight was about to start.

But no one moved forward, not even Irwin. Instead, he grinned like an asshole.

"Elijah, I'd like to introduce you to my new friends, the Guillory coven. I'm sure you've heard of them. They have quite a reputation."

"They do," Elijah confirmed. He wasn't looking at Irwin anymore but rather at the mages.

Terrence noticed several of them whispering under their breath and making small gestures with her hands. He tensed, knowing they were up to something. What was it? Were they going to pull down the gate with magic? To hurt everyone behind it? Maybe kill them?

"Considering their reputation, I want to give you one last chance to surrender," Irwin continued. "If you do, I won't kill all of your people. The coven wants only one thing, so they'll leave you alone when they have him. You'll die, but most of your dragons will survive. Isn't that what you want?" Irwin sounded smug and like he thought he'd already won.

He might have, but he hadn't counted on Gunther and Amelia both being here.

Terrence had seen them arrive. They came and went because Valerian needed training. Victor was taking care of his psychic training while Gunther and Amelia focused on the mage side. Gunther hadn't stopped helping, even when his coven had told him to. Since he was here today, Terrence wasn't as worried as he might have been otherwise.

But he still didn't know what the Guillory coven was up to, and he didn't like it.

One of the mages raised a hand. She was still murmuring, but her voice was louder. Terrence couldn't hear what she was saying because of the guards whispering around him, but he doubted that she was about to do something nice for the dragons.

The gate started shaking. It was as if a giant invisible hand was trying to pull it from the ground. Most of the people around Terrence took a step back, but Terrence stayed where he was. Donahue was whispering to someone who was invisible to Terrence, which had to mean that Kenneth was there. They needed all the help they could find, so it was a good thing.

The sensation of a heavy weight passed over Terrence. For a moment, he thought the Guillory coven had done something to him and the others standing with him, but when he looked at them, they appeared puzzled and angry. He understood why when Gunther stepped up to the gate to stand on Elijah's other side. Amelia was behind him, both of her hands raised.

Gunther flicked one of his hands, and the gate stopped shaking. He arched a brow, directing his attention to the mages instead of Irwin.

"You're going to have to do better than that," he drawled

as if he didn't have a care in the world. "I won't let you in."

"And if you do manage to get in, we'll fight you," Valerian declared. "I'd rather die than go with you. You didn't accept my parents or me before, so I know you don't have good intentions. If you did, you wouldn't be working with Irwin."

"Your place isn't with the dragons," a woman said, stepping forward. "I'm sorry about the way the coven treated you and your parents in the past, but it's over. We're your family, and we want you to come home."

Terrence snorted softly. Did she think Valerian would go with her if she asked nicely? She was obviously lying through her teeth. Everything about her felt fake, from her gentle tone to her concerned expression.

Valerian laughed. "Did you think I was going to believe that?"

"I don't see why you shouldn't. We *are* your family. Your grandparents were part of our coven. As was your father."

"You're not my family, and you never will be. You don't even *want* to be my family. If you did, you would have tried contacting me through Elijah, and you wouldn't be telling me that I belong with you when it's obvious I'm not going anywhere. I don't know why you need me when you were so disgusted by me in the past, but I don't care. I might not be as strong as your coven, but I'm not alone anymore. I have an entire dragon clan who will defend me, and I don't need anyone else."

Terrence wondered how things would end. Whatever the reason the coven wanted Valerian so desperately, it had to be important. He might have been willing to hear them out if they'd attempted to contact him, but instead, they'd gone to Irwin. That meant Valerian would rather die than go with them.

But Terrence would rather no one died except the bad guys. Irwin's name would be on top if he could make a list, but he'd make sure to put the coven members up there with him. They were doing this because they were selfish and wanted things that didn't belong to them. They yearned for power and to take over the dragon clan, but they hadn't counted on the dragons having allies like Gunther and Amelia.

They were only two mages, but Irwin and the Guillory coven didn't have to know that. As long as they believed they were backed by Gunther's coven, things would be all right.

For now, anyway. It would be fairly easy for them to find out that Gunther's coven wasn't happy with him, and when they did, they'd know that Gunther and Amelia were the only mages protecting the clan.

And the clan would be in trouble.

Donahue was proud of Valerian for standing up to Irwin and the people who had caused his family's death. He'd lost his parents because of the Guillory coven, and it couldn't be easy for him to face them like he was.

The woman who'd been talking to Valerian sneered. "You'll regret not coming with us today. We won't hesitate to kill every single one of your pet dragons."

Valerian crossed his arms over his chest. "You can try. But there's a reason you're here and want me so desperately, so I know you won't hurt me."

"We might not hurt you, but we can kill your family again."

Valerian stepped even closer to the gate, but Cooper stopped him with a hand on his shoulder. He pulled his boyfriend back, which was a relief. Valerian was strong but couldn't let that woman get to him.

Donahue could only imagine what Valerian had gone through. He'd lost his parents and had been on the run for most of his life. He'd finally found a place to call home where he could settle, and now, the coven was threatening him. It was a miracle he wasn't hiding in his bedroom, curled up in a corner with a blanket on his head to keep everyone and everything out. Donahue was in awe and wished he could be half as strong as Valerian.

Irwin seemed pissed, maybe because the woman had interrupted the conversation he'd been having with Elijah. It made Donahue wonder if the mages and the cockatrices would start fighting each other. Maybe they'd get distracted by each other and would forget about the dragons.

One could only hope.

"As I was saying," Irwin said loudly. "You can still save your clan. Hand over Valerian and open the gate. Let us in, and we won't kill everyone."

Elijah raised his phone. Donahue couldn't see what was on the screen since he was behind the alpha, but he *could* see Irwin's reaction to it. He went pale and even took a step back, staggering as if he'd seen a ghost.

He hadn't because he wasn't a psychic, but he was in shock anyway.

"When I found out you were coming, I called my journalist friend," Elijah drawled as if he didn't have a care in the world. "I put the phone on speaker so he could hear what was happening. He heard everything, and I'm sure he's already started writing his article. As I'm sure you're aware, he's well-known around here, so I have no doubt he'll find someone to publish it. By tomorrow, everyone in the city will know what happened today."

Irwin roared. He was angry, and Terrence remembered how he reacted when he was angry. He wasn't surprised to see Irwin shift.

Terrence reacted instinctively. It wasn't his place to protect Elijah. Elijah could protect himself, and if he shifted, he could take on Irwin. There was no way around the fact that Irwin was smaller than Elijah when they were both shifted. As long as it was a one-on-one fight, Elijah would win.

But Terrence didn't think about that when he placed himself in front of his new alpha. Irwin had been about to throw himself at the gate, but seeing Terrence made him pause. Terrence looked him in the eyes, raising his chin high.

"I won't let you hurt Elijah or anyone else," he said quietly. "You're not my alpha anymore, and I won't hesitate to fight you."

As long as it was only Irwin against Terrence, Terrence was pretty sure he could win. He was younger than Irwin and better trained. Irwin hadn't needed to defend himself in years. Everyone in the cockatrice clan was afraid of him, and they would never dare attack him. The guards were trained to defend their territory, though. Terrence knew what he was doing in a fight, and while Irwin might have, too, it had been years since he'd had to physically defend himself and his clan.

Irwin shifted back. Terrence was relieved, but he tried not to show it. He didn't want Irwin to see that he'd been worried.

"How dare you?" Irwin spat out. "I housed and fed your family for decades, and this is how you repay me? You take my son's fiancé away and give her to the dragons?"

Terrence was disgusted. "I didn't take away your son's fiancé. I took away my teenage sister, whom you were forcing to marry your son. I didn't *give* her to anyone. She's free to live her life how she wants, and she is."

Terrence had been watching both Gunther and Amelia and the mages on the other side of the gate. There was a silent battle happening between them. They were all murmuring and gesturing, and most of them had their hands raised.

Terrence had expected something more impressive. They were fighting with magic, yet he couldn't see anything. He could still feel the strange weight he'd felt earlier, but that was it.

The woman who'd spoken to Valerian earlier moved closer to Irwin. She touched his back, and even though he shrugged her hand off, he nodded.

"This isn't over," he threatened. "I gave you one last chance to do the right thing. You didn't take it, which means everyone here will die."

"You can try," Valerian snapped. "But you'll find we're more powerful than you think." He glanced at the woman. "You all will."

Irwin shifted back to his cockatrice form and pushed himself into the air. Terrence tensed, expecting him to fly over the gate, but instead, his old alpha turned and flew away. The Guillory coven members finally dropped their hands and quickly climbed onto the cockatrice shifters. Terrence stayed where he was until all of them had vanished from sight.

"That was weird," Donahue said. "What were they doing with all the whispering and shit?"

"Trying to take down the gate with magic," Gunther told him. He raked a hand through his hair. "They were planning to attack. I'd put a protective spell on the gate a while ago, and I'm glad I did. It slowed them down, and Amelia and I were able to put a new spell on the gate and keep a shield over all of us. I don't think it's over, though." He turned to Elijah. "This was a test. They wanted to see if you had mages and how strong we are. Now, they know. They're going to plan accordingly, and it might be a problem. Amelia and I are strong, but the Guillory coven has more people, and they're just as strong, if not stronger."

Terrence suspected that if it had been up to Irwin, the cockatrices would have attacked today, but Irwin wasn't in this alone. He had to deal with the Guillory coven, and Terrence wondered if this visit was because of the mages. If what Gunther was saying was right and they'd wanted to see how many mages were here and what they were capable of, they'd given them exactly what they'd been looking for.

Now, the Guillory coven knew about Gunther and Amelia. They knew that Valerian wasn't going back to them, no matter how nicely they asked.

They knew they had a real fight on their hands, and Terrence had no doubt they were taking it seriously, even if Irwin wasn't. The next time the cockatrices and the Guillory coven came, it wouldn't be for a conversation and a few threats.

It would be for a war.

CHAPTER THIRTEEN

It had been a week, and nothing had happened. Terrence wasn't sure what was worse—having to wonder when the cockatrices would attack or them attacking so they could get this war out of the way. Right now, waiting was what annoyed Terrence the most. He hated not knowing what would happen next, and he wanted Irwin to make a decision. In the meantime, everyone was tense and hypervigilant.

He speared a potato from his plate but wasn't hungry. He was too worried to eat.

People had started snapping at each other. There had been several brawls in the house, usually over stupid things like who had eaten the last meatball. It was ridiculous, but the tension was pushing all of them to the end of their patience, and things wouldn't get better until Irwin finally did something.

Terrence was proud of the way he'd stood up to his old alpha, but having Irwin vanish made him nervous. He hoped it meant that the cockatrices and the mages were fighting, but it would be too good to be true.

The dragons needed more mages. Gunther had left last week promising to talk to his coven, and while he might have called Elijah, Terrence was worried because no one else seemed to have heard from him. Had something happened? Was his coven keeping him away from the clan?

"Can you pass me the potatoes?" Donahue asked.

Terrence smiled at him. Donahue was the one bright thing in Terrence's world. Now that they were more comfortable here, Terrence and his family weren't spending as much time together as they used to. While Terrence, Joe, and their father were building their own spaces, Natasha already had her own life, friends, and things to do. They were still there for each other, but spending time with other people was odd. Before, they'd only had each other. Now, Terrence had Donahue and his family and was making friends. Joe was still a bit closed off, but Terrence had noticed that he'd started talking to people, which he hadn't been sure would happen.

Even though things were getting complicated, Terrence's life and his family were settling, and it was good. He didn't know what he'd do if he lost that because of Irwin, and he hoped he wouldn't have to find out.

He glanced around the table. Not every clan member was here, but many were, eating dinner and talking. Terrence's father was talking to the woman who'd been recently attacked. Terrence had found out that her name was Heloise and that the cockatrices had hurt her badly. He felt guilty, even though he hadn't been involved.

Elijah was there, too. He was talking to Jerome, and their expressions were grim, but that was often the case for them. Jerome especially was a grumpy person, even when he was with his boyfriend.

The front door opened and closed, but no one paid attention to it. It was normal with clan members coming and going. Terrence looked up when the person walked into the dining room and smiled when he saw it was Gunther. He knew he'd been right to be worried when he saw Gunther's expression.

"I can't believe it," he declared as he went to flop on an empty chair. He wasn't far from Elijah on the other side of the table, and he got the alpha's attention right away.

"What happened?" Elijah asked.

"I spent the past week trying to convince my coven leader to take your side in this fight. I pointed out that if the dragons lose, it'll be a disaster for the entire supernatural community in the city, including the coven. Irwin won't stop for anything to get what he wants, and I wouldn't be surprised if he started attacking other clans and supernatural groups once he's done with the dragons, but they don't believe it. They think that if they stay out of this, Irwin will ignore them if he wins. They refuse to look at the future and threatened to lock me up if I continue visiting."

"Yet you're here," Donahue pointed out.

"I told them to fuck off and that I'd do what I want. At this point, I wish I weren't part of the coven."

Donahue grimaced. "Can't you leave?"

Gunther rubbed his face. "I could, but where would I go? The only work I've ever done was through the coven. People reach out, and the coven leader chooses who's better suited for the job. I'd have to find clients, an apartment, and earn enough money for the supplies. I wouldn't know where to start, and I hate that. I've never lived on my own, but it's never been a problem until now."

"You could become a clan member."

Gunther looked at Donahue as if he'd said something unexpected, but Terrence was pretty sure that anyone listening to him right now had thought the same thing.

It seemed kind of obvious. Why couldn't Gunther be a clan member? He already spent a lot of time here, both because he was training Valerian and because he was a close friend of Elijah's. From everything Terrence had heard about Gunther's coven, he was surprised Gunther hadn't become a clan member sooner.

Maybe he didn't want to be one. Amelia had said she liked her freedom and had refused to become a clan member, and while Terrence could understand, he'd rather be protected and surrounded by people he considered family. Of course, Amelia was a mage, while he was a shifter. Shifters almost always lived in big groups from birth, but Terrence didn't think the same went for mages. They also didn't have an animal side that needed that kind of community.

"I can't become a clan member," Gunther said.

"Why not?" Elijah asked from his side of the table. "You already spend a lot of time here. You've even stayed the night several times. You know the clan and its people. You get along with most of them, and we could use another mage."

"I'm not a dragon."

Terrence snorted loudly. "In case you haven't noticed, I'm not a dragon, and neither is Donahue. We're still clan members."

They wouldn't have been if Elijah had been any other alpha. Terrence had never heard of a group of shifters welcoming people who weren't the same species, let alone humans. They hired them if they needed a mage, but the mage didn't become part of the group.

But Elijah was an unusual alpha, and this clan was an unusual clan. Terrence had never thought it would be possible for dragons and cockatrices to live together, but they were, and no one had died. No one had even bled. Joe had bickered with a few dragons, but thankfully, he'd realized it was better to step away before things got out of hand.

Everyone was looking at Elijah now. The alpha didn't seem to care. He was as relaxed as he'd been before, and his focus was on Gunther. A smile played on his lips, and he appeared almost satisfied for some reason.

Maybe he'd wanted Gunther to become a clan member but hadn't found the right moment to ask. It was never easy to decide to leave people you'd lived with for so long. It had even been complicated for Terrence, who'd hated living with the cockatrices and Irwin.

"You're telling me that I can be a clan member?" Gunther asked with his attention on Elijah now.

"You only have to ask."

For a moment, the room was silent. Everyone waited for Gunther's decision. Terrence already knew what he'd choose and grinned when Gunther nodded. "All right. I'm asking, then. Can I become a clan member even though I'm a mage?"

Elijah beamed. "Welcome to the clan, Gunther."

Maybe it was because he hadn't been a clan member for that long, but Donahue didn't understand why everyone was so surprised at the thought of Gunther becoming a clan member. It made sense, whichever way one thought about it.

Gunther wasn't happy with his coven. He'd been telling everyone who would listen about them and the fucked-up decisions they made. He tried to convince them that helping the dragons was the smartest thing to do, but Donahue suspected they wouldn't change their mind. They were trying to protect themselves, and he understood why they wanted distance from the clan, but they should know better. This wouldn't end well if Irwin won, and that was something everyone should keep in mind when they decided which side they wanted to be on.

There wasn't a neutral side. As far as Donahue was concerned, staying out of it meant being on Irwin's side. Elijah wouldn't retaliate if he won, but he'd keep in mind who hadn't supported the clan, and when they needed help, he would act accordingly. It was a pity that Gunther was losing the place he'd called home for so long, but he wouldn't be alone. He had plenty of friends here, and Donahue thought he'd be okay.

The problem was that it might turn Gunther's coven into an enemy, and they couldn't afford to have more of that. He didn't want to bring down the mood, so he kept those thoughts to himself. He was sure Elijah had thought of it, anyway. The alpha always thought about everything, or at least, that was what it felt like. Elijah knew what he was doing, and if he thought that Gunther becoming a coven member was a good idea, then it was.

"My coven won't be happy," Gunther warned.

He'd already agreed to be a clan member, but it looked like he might not have thought about all the implications until now, or maybe he had but wanted to make sure Elijah knew about it.

"I don't think they've ever been happy about anything when it comes to the clan," Elijah told him.

"Well, no, but even though they're not as strong as the Guillory coven, you can't afford to make them your enemy. I don't want them on Irwin's side. We wouldn't have a chance to win with two covens working with him."

"They're afraid of Irwin. They want to stay as far from him as possible, which is why they refused to help us. I can't be a hundred percent sure, but I doubt they'll do something as stupid as working with Irwin. Even if they decide to work with him, we can find a way around them thanks to you."

"Don't count on that. I'll step in if they do something stupid, but I don't want to hurt them. Besides, the entire coven didn't get to decide. Only the elders did, and the leader approved. It wouldn't be fair to punish people who want to help us but can't."

"What do you think about talking to them?" Donahue asked.

Gunther frowned and looked at him. "What do you mean?"

"You're the only one who has strong ties to our clan, but you might not be the only one who wants to help or believes that the coven is making the wrong decision. We all know we need more mages because no matter how strong you and Amelia are, there are only two of you. Maybe other members of your coven will want to help."

"If they do, they'll be kicked out of the coven."

"Will they? How many times has your coven threatened to kick you out? Because I always hear you complain about that, but you still come around. It looks to me like they're trying to control your behavior, but they're not willing to push so hard that they'll lose you." The joke was on them because Gunther had left anyway.

Donahue doubted that most of the other coven members would be willing to leave to help the clan, but they didn't have to become clan members. As long as the coven didn't kick them out because they wanted to help, there shouldn't be a problem.

"It's something to think about," Elijah said.

He nodded at Donahue. Donahue felt ridiculously happy at the thought he might have helped the clan. It wasn't much, but they desperately needed mages, and apart from Gunther and Amelia, Donahue couldn't think of anyone who could convince them to help.

He looked around the table. He cared about the people sitting here and didn't want to lose any of them. He probably would. As long as Irwin was bent on taking over the clan, people would get hurt. No one would back down from protecting the clan, but they all knew it wouldn't come without sacrifices.

It scared Donahue. He'd found a new place to call home, and he liked it. He could see himself in the future, living with the clan and loving Terrence. The thought that he might lose all of it before it happened made him want to scream. It meant he'd have to work harder to protect it.

He couldn't shift into a dragon, and he couldn't use magic, but that didn't mean he was useless.

He leaned back in his chair, his mind working. The only ability Donahue had was that he could talk to ghosts. He wanted to be useful in the upcoming war, and he'd been trying to find a way, but just helping with Kenneth didn't feel like enough.

But what if he helped with more ghosts?

Irwin had been the cockatrice alpha for a long time. He didn't like people not obeying his every order, so Donahue was ready to bet that if someone opposed him, Irwin got rid of them. He might kick them out of the clan, but Donahue wouldn't be surprised to find out he killed his opponents and anyone who tried standing up to him. Not all of these people would stay back as ghosts, but what if enough of them had? What if Donahue and the other psychics could use the ghosts against Irwin in some way?

Donahue didn't know if it was possible, but he was excited at the thought of actually helping. It would take some work, and it might be dangerous if they had to sneak into cockatrice territory to find ghosts, but he was willing to do anything to protect the clan and its people.

The clan was his future, and if he wanted to have one, he'd need to work hard to save it.

CHAPTER FOURTEEN

Terrence couldn't find his phone, but he was pretty sure he'd left it in the living room. He'd looked everywhere else, and it wasn't in his room or the kitchen, the two rooms where he spent the most time. That left only the living room and Donahue's bedroom, but before going there, he wanted to check if it was on the coffee table.

Everyone in the house was anxious, but after Elijah had made Gunther a clan member, people had relaxed a bit. They still needed more mages, but having Gunther and Amelia on their side helped. They wouldn't be enough to stand up to the Guillory coven, but for now, this tiny step in the right direction made everyone feel better. Irwin was no doubt still plotting against them, but he'd been quiet, and Terrence wanted to enjoy it because it wouldn't last.

He pushed open the living room door and walked in, already looking in the direction of the coffee table. His attention didn't stay on it for more than a few seconds because it caught on two people kissing on the couch.

It took Terrence a moment to make sense of what he was seeing. The couple kissing was entwined together. One of them was a blonde woman who had her hands buried in the hair of the man she was kissing.

The other was his father.

They didn't spring apart like teenagers who'd been caught doing something they shouldn't. When they heard Terrence, they moved back, and while Terrence's father's eyes widened, he didn't rush into an explanation. He and Terrence stared at each other for a moment, and Terrence tried to make sense of how he felt.

He rubbed his face. "I could have done without seeing that," he muttered.

"You were the one who walked in on us," his father pointed out.

Now that Terrence could see both of them in the face, he recognized the woman as Heloise. He'd noticed his father was spending a lot of time with her, but he'd thought it was because he felt guilty about the cockatrices hurting her. Terrence did, even though he hadn't had anything to do with the attack.

Clearly, there had been more to it than feeling guilty.

"I thought I left my phone here, and yep, there it is." Terrence snatched it from the coffee table and waved it around like an idiot. "I'll just go."

"*I* should go," Heloise said as she got to her feet. "The two of you need to talk."

She looked as uncomfortable as Terrence felt, and while Terrence wanted this to be over as soon as possible, he thought it would be best if he told both his father and Heloise how he felt about this.

"It's fine," he told her. "I'm a bit horrified, but that's because he's my dad. I don't have anything against the two of you dating. If you make my dad happy, I'm all for it. As long as you don't expect me to call you Mom."

Heloise looked horrified. "Please, don't."

Terrence laughed. "I promise I never will. But seriously. I don't know you well, but my father deserves happiness. I don't care that you're a dragon shifter or younger than him. It's none of my business."

"I'll never forget your mother," Terrence's father said. "But it's been a long time."

Terrence wanted to run away screaming, but this was an

important conversation. "I never expected you to forget Mom, but I also don't expect you to be alone for the rest of your life. I'm an adult, and so are you. You can do whatever you want, even if I disagree with it, but in this case, I don't. We were given a chance at a new life. It would be stupid to waste it."

"I'm happy this went the right way, but you two have plans tonight," Heloise said.

It took a moment for Terrence to remember why he'd been looking for his phone. He and his family were having dinner with Donahue's brothers and parents. They all lived in the same house, but it was so big and so many people shared it that it was easy to avoid people, even not on purpose. With Donahue and Terrence being together, their families had wanted to meet, and Terrence was excited.

Natasha already loved Donahue's mother. Terrence was a bit afraid the woman wouldn't like him for her son, but he was pretty sure that Donahue didn't need her approval. He'd be with Terrence even if she hated him, but that didn't mean Terrence didn't want to make a good impression or that he didn't want Donahue's family to like him.

"You could come with us," he offered.

Heloise shook her head. "I like your father, and we're together, but it's too soon for that kind of dinner. Besides, I already know Donahue's family. This dinner is for you and your family to get to know them."

"But we'll have dinner together soon, right?" If Heloise was someone his father wanted to be with, then Terrence wanted to get to know her.

Her smile was gentle and sweet. "Of course."

Terrence looked at his father. "I'm picking Donahue up at his bedroom. I'll see you at dinner?"

"Yes." He looked relieved, as if he'd expected Terrence to pick a fight or throw a tantrum.

Terrence wasn't even tempted to. His mother had died a

long time ago, and while he would always love her memory, he wasn't surprised that his father needed to move on. It had been too long since he'd allowed himself to have something for himself. He'd protected his children from Irwin as best as he could and had ignored his own needs. He didn't have to anymore, though.

None of them did.

Terrence left them to say their goodbyes and headed upstairs. Even though he wasn't eager to think about his father kissing anyone, he was smiling like an idiot. He wanted his entire family to be as happy as he was with Donahue, and this felt like the first step. Natasha was nowhere near old enough to have a serious relationship, but maybe Joe would find love here, just like Terrence and their father had.

He was still smiling when he knocked on Donahue's door. Donahue opened it almost instantly, then looked him up and down. "You look good," he said, even though Terrence wore dark jeans and a button-up shirt.

"You look good, too," Terrence said. Donahue was wearing pretty much the same, but this wasn't a formal dinner. It was just a meeting between two families who already knew each other.

"And you're smiling."

Terrence grinned. "That's because I'm happy to see you, but also because I walked in on my father kissing someone."

Donahue's eyes widened. "Really? Can you tell me about it?"

"I don't see why I shouldn't. He's serious about her, and you're part of the family." Terrence's heart felt bigger at that thought.

Donahue *was* part of his family, and maybe Heloise would become part of it soon. He'd been terrified when he'd decided to tell the dragons about the Guillory coven, but it had been the best thing he could have done for himself and his family.

He'd never regret it, even if the dragons lost this war.

They wouldn't. Terrence would make sure of that. He didn't know how yet, but he couldn't let Irwin win.

Dinner was a hit. Donahue had been a bit nervous, even though he knew it would be fine. Since they all lived in the same house, they knew each other. This wasn't a meeting-the-family dinner, but rather, a getting-to-know-the-family dinner.

And it was going well.

Everyone around the table was smiling and eating and of course, talking. Unfortunately, the war with the cockatrices was the main topic of the conversations. There was nothing to be done about that, and Donahue didn't mind. He *wanted* to talk about the upcoming fight. The more they did, the more probable it was that they'd find a solution.

"We need more mages," Victor declared.

Tim, his boyfriend, was sitting next to him. He was part of the family, too, and things were a bit tight around the table. If Olsen, Roslin, and Joe all found partners, this small dining room would be too small for all of them. They might have to use the main dining room, which meant they'd have to work around the rest of the clan.

But that was a problem to think about after they won the fight.

"Gunther is looking into it," Donahue said. "But from what he said, people are wary of the Guillory coven. They have a bad reputation."

"What kind of reputation? Everyone keeps saying that, but no one explains."

"I've heard about them," Roslin said. "A client told me a few things. They're ruthless in what they want and don't hesitate to take out smaller covens if they stand in their way."

That made them sound like mass murderers. Donahue wouldn't be surprised if they were. After all, they'd allied with a man who was notorious for killing his rivals and anyone who stood up to him. If he'd been human, the justice system would have stepped in long ago. Irwin *wasn't* human, though. He was a shifter, and humans tended to stay away from them and what they considered shifter problems.

That was why so many alphas and leaders got away with killing their people. It was horrible, but there was little anyone could do.

"I might know people who can help, but it's complicated," Olsen said.

He looked down at his plate. Donahue wanted to ask him what he meant, but it was clear that he needed a moment.

Eventually, he straightened. "Family dinner probably isn't the right time to do this."

"You don't have to talk about it if you don't want to," their mother said, reaching over the table to pat his hand.

"I know. I think I might be able to help, though, and I want to."

Olsen cleared his throat and looked around the table. Donahue smiled, hoping to reassure him. Everything would be okay, no matter what Olsen had to say.

"You know I've always felt out of place and like I don't quite belong," he explained. "It's nothing anyone did. It's just how it is because I'm not a psychic in a family of psychics. I don't hate any of you for having an ability I don't have, but since I've always felt a bit left out, I made friends with a bunch of people who feel like me. For one reason or another, they don't quite belong with the people they live with. Most of them are hybrids, which means they're not welcome in the shifter groups they were born in."

Donahue hated that Olsen felt this way, but he wasn't sure there was anything anyone could do about it. They couldn't fix Olsen because there was nothing wrong with him. He was human and hadn't gotten a drop of psychic blood. No one could change that.

Donahue would in a heartbeat if he could, and maybe there was someone out there — maybe a mage — who could turn Olsen into a psychic. He doubted that was the case. Psychics were born that way, and Olsen hadn't been.

"Do you know where these people live?" Victor asked.

"Most of them are in the area. It's a local group."

"What kind of hybrids are we talking about?"

No one here cared about that beyond the fact that it could help them defeat Irwin. Valerian was a hybrid, after all, and everyone loved him.

"The group is pretty big, so there's a bit of everything, from mages to psychics and shifters. I don't think all of them would help, but some will want to."

"Will they want something in exchange?" Terrence asked. "Maybe to become clan members? Because it sounds like they're trying to find a place where they belong like you are."

"I already found a place where I belong, but you're right. They yearn for a place to call home, and they might decide to help if they know the clan will welcome them once this is over. I can't make promises, though."

"No one expects you to," Donahue reassured his brother. "It's great that you came up with this opportunity, and I think you need to talk to Elijah."

"You don't think it's stupid?"

"You might be giving us a bunch of allies we never expected. I don't see why anyone should have a problem with it."

Even if Olsen's online friends weren't particularly powerful, they could still help. Elijah had a soft heart, and Donahue suspected he'd want to do something for these people even if they decided to stay out of the fight. Donahue didn't know if he'd do the same, but there was a reason he wasn't the alpha.

Olsen's friends might not win them the war, but if even one of them could help, they'd have more possibilities to win this.

As Donahue looked around the table, he had the certainty that this was what mattered. The clan would fight to protect their friends and families, and since now the clan included a bunch of psychics, they would, too. Donahue wouldn't let anyone take away his home or his family.

Not even one member of it.

EPILOGUE

Movie night had become a tradition for Terrence. The dragons loved gathering in the living room, piling up on the couches and armchairs, and spending a few hours not thinking about Irwin and the war. They ate popcorn and snacks and spent time together, and it was great. It helped to not obsess over what was happening with Irwin.

No one knew what he was up to. Kenneth was still sneaking around, but either Irwin had finally realized they were using a ghost to spy on him, or the mages were more careful than he'd ever been, because Kenneth couldn't find much information. Everyone in the cockatrice clan was still terrified of Irwin, and he was angrier than ever, but he hadn't attacked yet. Terrence knew he was plotting something, and he desperately wished he knew what, but only Irwin did. He didn't trust anyone and wouldn't tell even his closest advisors.

But that wasn't what Terrence wanted to think about tonight. He snuggled closer to Donahue and leaned his head against his boyfriend's shoulder, breathing in and out a few times until he felt more relaxed.

It was Olsen's turn to choose the movie tonight, and he'd picked one with a gorgeous blonde woman who decided to be a lawyer and excelled at it, even though no one expected her to. It made Terrence think of himself a bit. He wasn't blond and didn't own a Chihuahua, but no one had expected him to get away from Irwin. He had, and he couldn't have been happier.

The sound of someone ringing at the gate made all of them

jump. It wasn't that late, but it was February, which meant it was dark outside. It wasn't Terrence's job to find out who was at the gate, but he was curious, so he kept an ear on the movie and one on the entrance to see if he could find out what was happening.

He hadn't expected much, but when he heard two guards whisper and one of them say she was getting Elijah, he knew something was up. Knowing his boyfriend would follow, he extracted himself from Donahue's arms and headed toward the front door. He got there at the same time as Elijah, so he was able to listen to the conversation between the alpha and the guard.

"Who did she say she is?" Elijah asked.

"She said her name is Elvira and that she needs to talk to you."

Terrence sucked in a breath. She couldn't be that bold, could she?

Elijah heard him and turned. "You know who she is?"

"I can't be sure until I see her, but that's Curt's mother's name."

Elijah's eyebrows shut up. "Curt's mother? Why would she be here?"

"She didn't take it well when Irwin killed her son." Terrence didn't think any mother would, and even though Curt had been an awful person, he'd still been Elvira's son.

"I can imagine," Elijah murmured. "But why is she here?"

"I was present during a meeting between her and Irwin. She was angry, and while she bent to Irwin's will, she clearly wanted revenge. She wants Irwin to pay for what he did to her son."

"Maybe she believes we can help her with that." Elijah turned and nodded at the guards. "Let her in, but keep her outside. I don't want her in the house."

The guards quickly left. Terrence wasn't sure what Elijah

expected of him, so he stayed where he was, his mind spinning. What was happening? Could Elvira want to ally with the dragons? Even if she did, what could she bring to the table that would help them defeat Irwin?

Donahue wrapped an arm around Terrence's shoulders. "Everything will be all right. I promise. I'm not going anywhere, whatever happens."

Even though they were just words, Terrence was reassured. More than the words, it was the presence of Donahue that made him feel better. Having his psychic here with him was worth a thousand words.

"I'd like you two to meet her with me," Elijah said. "Terrence, you already know her, so your insight will be precious."

"Why do you want *me* there?" Donahue asked.

Elijah looked amused. "Because you'd ask to be there anyway since Terrence will be present. I'd rather not fight you."

Terrence snickered. Elijah was right. If Donahue had his way, he and Terrence would never spend more than fifteen minutes apart. Their relationship was new, and knowing that one or both of them could be hurt or worse when Irwin finally attacked meant they were attached at the hips. For now, that was perfectly fine with Terrence.

The door opened again, and one of the guards peeked in. She nodded, and Terrence watched as Elijah went from being a friend to being the alpha.

He squared his shoulders, straightened his back, and raised his chin. He might be wearing jeans and a sweater, but his authority was clear. No one would doubt he was the alpha.

Terrence and Donahue followed him outside. Donahue hovered close by, but he gave Terrence enough space to move. Even though Terrence knew Elvira was waiting for them, he was still stunned at the sight. She'd come here with only two men, apparently not afraid that the dragons would hurt her.

She was a beautiful woman, even in her early sixties. Her hair was dark, and while Terrence knew it couldn't be natural, it suited her. She wore makeup, a pair of jeans under a jacket, and high-heeled boots. Her expression was defiant, but she was here for a reason, and Terrence couldn't wait to find out what that reason was.

"I'd like to know why you're here," Elijah said.

"To make you an offer you shouldn't refuse."

"What offer?"

Her gaze flickered to Terrence. "I'm sure you know what Irwin did to my son. I want him to pay for that. No matter how much of an asshole Curt was, he didn't deserve to die just because Irwin was angry at him."

Terrence didn't think that was why Curt had deserved to die, but he kept his mouth shut. Either Curt's mother already knew what a bad person he'd been, or she was ignoring it. Terrence didn't think anything would change her mind when it came to her son, especially now that Curt was dead.

"What are you offering?" Elijah asked. "Because I only see you and two men. I don't trust you, so if this is all you have, I'll have to say no."

Elvira's jaw tightened, and Terrence expected her to say something nasty. Instead, she sucked in a breath. "I have more than these two men," she said. "More than half the cockatrice clan wants Irwin to stop. They don't want to die, and they see how foolish all of this is. Irwin is the only one who wants to gain more power and to defeat you. If I step up and take my nephew's place as the alpha, I'll keep this war from happening."

Terrence blinked. He hadn't expected that, but he wasn't surprised. It was time someone defeated Irwin and took his place as the alpha, but he wasn't sure Elvira was the right choice.

"You want me to make you the cockatrice alpha?"

"I want to fight on your side and avoid this war. If that means killing my nephew, I'll do it. He deserves it after what he did to my son, and with him gone, the cockatrices will leave you alone."

"I need to think about it and talk to my people," Elijah said. "And I still don't trust you."

Elvira chuckled. "I don't trust you, either, but the enemy of my enemy is my friend and all that. If being allied with you means that Irwin will pay for killing my son, I'm all for it." She took out a piece of paper from her jacket pocket and handed it to Elijah. "This is my number. Call me when you've made your decision, but don't wait too long. Irwin is working with that coven, and eventually, they'll have enough of wasting time. In the meantime, I'll start talking to people and try to get as many as I can on our side. One way or another, Irwin will lose."

Terrence wished he could be as confident as Elvira.

She turned to leave, and everyone was silent until the gate closed behind the car in which she'd arrived with her two bodyguards. Even after she was gone, Terrence could feel the tension.

"What do you think of this?" Elijah asked. "You're the one who knows her best."

"I wouldn't trust her, but she's right. We need help. She knows Irwin better than anyone, even me. She also has a personal reason to want him dead, so I feel we might have to take this chance."

"I'll ask Kenneth to keep an eye on her," Donahue interjected. "When she comes back, he can follow her and listen to her conversations. That way, we'll know what she's up to."

The dragons needed allies, but they had to be sure those people wouldn't stab them in the back. Terrence didn't know if Elvira had a goal beyond making Irwin pay and becoming the cockatrice alpha, but if she did, they'd find out soon.

ABOUT THE AUTHOR

Catherine is the creator of several series, most of them paranormal, including the Whitedell Pride Series and the Gillham Pack Series. While she graduated in translation, she decided to go the writer's way because it was more fun to create her own stories and characters.

She's been living in Italy for more than twenty years, but she's a daughter of the North—Belgium to be precise—and she misses it so much that she's already planning to move back.

She loves pizza—probably too much—her son, her pets, and of course, books. She sneaks some reading time into her schedule every time she has five minutes free from writing, demands from her various pets and son, and lastly, housework.

Connect with her:

lievens.catherine@gmail.com
BookBub: https://www.bookbub.com/authors/catherine-lievens
Website: https://authorcatherinelievens.com/
Facebook: https://www.facebook.com/catherine.lievens.9
Facebook Group: https://www.facebook.com/groups/411788002341528/
Twitter: https://twitter.com/authorCLievens
Newsletter: http://eepurl.com/c-uvKn